He grasped her hand and brought it to his lips.
His kiss was so delicate, she almost fainted on the spot. The touch of his skin on hers was warm, light, and inviting. She imagined how his lips would feel on the rest of her body. What was going on with her? Was she losing the tenuous grip she had on her sanity?

"No, Lily," he said. "The pleasure was all mine." He paused for a moment. "Would you like to have dinner with me tonight? Unless of course you have other plans and have to head back home."

Lily hesitated. She had been on a few casual dates since her divorce six months earlier, but she had never been asked out by a complete stranger. Sympathetic friends, just trying to help her get on with her life, set up most of the one-date-only events she had attended. But none of the nice yet ordinary men made her feel the way she did right now.

Electricity crackled between them. She was certain they had a strong, unexplained connection even if her rational side was telling her it wasn't a smart idea to get involved with this guy.

In Pursuit of Paradise

by

Kate Randle

In Pursuit of Paradise

Cover Art by *Kristian Norris*

The Wild Rose Press, Inc.
PO Box 708
Adams Basin, NY 14410-0708
Visit us at www.thewildrosepress.com

Publishing History
First Champagne Rose Edition, 2017
Print ISBN 978-1-5092-1157-9
Digital ISBN 978-1-5092-1158-6

Published in the United States of America

Dedications

I dedicate this novel to my wonderful husband Jason
and my two children.
At every twist and turn in this incredible voyage,
they have helped me make my dreams come true.

~*~

A big thank-you also goes out to my personal fabulous
five: Joni, Kim, Krista, Rachel, and Stephanie.
This amazing group of women read endlessly,
critiqued tirelessly, and kept me focused throughout
this extraordinary journey.

~*~

And to my readers, thank-you for taking the time
to enjoy *In Pursuit of Paradise*.
I hope you love reading Nick and Lily's story
as much as I loved writing it.

Chapter One

Nicholas Becket was having a bad day…a very bad day. Just yesterday, he had promised his family, his father in particular, that he was going to try harder. Given the present circumstances, he needed to man up and take some responsibility for his family and the Becket Empire. This had not been his usual pattern in life so far. However, after that heartfelt meeting, he found himself in a nightclub just down the street from where he was now.

That was pretty much all Nick remembered, until he woke up this morning with that bombshell redhead in his bed. He was late again, because he had spent half the night partying with this gorgeous stranger. And of course, setting his alarm clock had been the furthest thing from his mind.

He rushed through a shower, shaved, and donned his uniform. With one final tug of his jacket sleeves, he approached the bed and shook the girl's shoulder. When she was awake, he told her to go home. Nick was going to change his ways. Starting right now.

As he ran down the hallway toward the hotel conference room, his thoughts were a jumbled mess. He was supposed to be organized, professional, and prepared for the task ahead. Yet, at this moment, he felt like none of those things.

As he reached his destination, he slowed to a walk,

took a deep breath, and ran his hands through his cropped dark blond hair. He then entered the vast meeting room. A large display indicated the sign-in table was located to the left of the entrance. He followed the directions and approached the area. The young brunette at the desk was pretty and dressed in a black suit with a very short skirt. She smiled up at him with an enticing grin and a knowing gleam in her eye.

"Good morning, Captain Becket," she said. "Can I help you?"

Nick groaned inwardly. She had recognized him, and he had no idea who she was. He was going to unstick himself from this destructive pattern, just as he'd promised his family he would. He tried to muster up his most professional façade.

"Good morning," he said. He was not going to give in to his urge to charm this woman. The days of using his handsome face and sly grin to get his way were in the past. Instead, he gave her a hard stare. "Could you please direct me to my section?"

"Of course." She was all businesslike, no longer the flirty woman he had approached. Thank goodness. She got up without another word and led him down the corridor to a row of tables set up for the interviews.

****

The first Saturday in August dawned a beautiful sunny summer day in central Florida. The weather had been perfect for the short drive Lily Kingston had taken to Cape Canaveral. She wasn't sure if she had been successful in getting what she wanted from this trip, but she was optimistic. At least she survived the interview. They had never been her strong suit. Anxiety always made her clam up and not come across as the strong, confident woman she once was. She couldn't be sure if she had gotten the position, but she did better than she had expected.

Last week, she received an email about a cruise ship job fair being held today. She had checked out the website and registered online. The Caribbean Paradise Cruise Line was launching their new ship, the Moonlight Queen, next month. It was just the thing Lily had been looking for, and the timing was perfect. At the age of thirty-two, fed up with her current job, life situation, and apartment, she needed a change, and the sooner, the better.

The artists' renderings of the ship were beautiful and the ports-of-call sounded exhilarating. There were many on-board activities for the crew, including special events such as movie nights and dance parties. The ship had several dining halls and a pool for employees. There were also shops, a casino, a gym, and a disco lounge. It had all the comforts of home and none of the problems. It would be long hours and a lot of hard work, but she was up for the challenge and a change of scenery would be most welcome for her.

Lily had just finished her interview with the recruitment administrator. Since she had no plans for the rest of the day, she wandered around the room looking at the various exhibits the company had set up. It was a chance to familiarize herself with the ship and a good way to stretch her legs before the long drive home. The space was elegant with large windows that looked out onto a stunning view of the hotel pool. The rose-colored walls were soft and calming to her frayed nerves. The oak tables and chairs scattered around the room looked expensive.

She admired the photographs and sketches that showed off the ship's stunning features. Lily was surprised to find that cruise ship life looked like a lot more fun than she expected. There were photos of crew members dressed in uniforms greeting passengers. Other pictures showed the staff relaxing in their quarters and dancing at the disco. It looked grand and foreign at the same time. Excitement rippled through her as she took in the various scenes. She took her time exploring the displays.

She was staring at a large poster of the ship as she was walking when without warning, she crashed head-on into something, no someone. During her stumble backwards, her purse and portfolio went flying, scattering her resume, notes, and other papers everywhere. A strong arm reached around her waist, steadying her.

"Oh, I'm so sorry…" Lily said as she looked up into the most beautiful piercing blue eyes she had ever seen. They were the color of a clear sparkling ocean. The arm around her waist was firm and muscular, radiating heat. She was so close to him, she could smell the spicy scent of his aftershave, and her stomach tightened with embarrassment or lust, she couldn't tell which. She was a bit dizzy from the sudden rush of sensory input. Trying in vain to regain her composure, she tried to speak but couldn't find her voice. Heat rose in her face, and her cheeks were no doubt bright red as they often were when she was embarrassed like she was at this moment.

"No, it's my fault." His voice was deep and very sexy. "I wasn't looking where I was going. Here, let me help you pick up your papers." He loosened his grip on her waist, and when she was standing upright again, he released her.

As the tall stranger bent down and gathered her things, Lily stared, dumbfounded. This man was gorgeous and wearing some kind of naval uniform. He had short blond hair. What would it be like to run her hands through it? Could the strands be as silky soft as she imagined? She shook her head and tried to focus.

"You must be Lily," he said, as he glanced at her resume.

"Yes," she stammered, as she managed to speak, although not very well. But before she could stop herself, she babbled on. "I was just interviewed for a job on the cruise ship." Then without thinking, she went on. "Are you here for an interview as well?"

"No," the man said and flashed her a breathtaking smile. His beautiful white teeth and full sensuous lips made Lily weak in the knees.

"I'm the captain of the Moonlight Queen and am here hiring officers for the ship. Some of the recruiters couldn't make it today. I had some experience in human resources before pursuing my degree in marine engineering, so I volunteered to help out by conducting interviews."

"Oh. Of course," she said. With his crisp white uniform and commanding presence, he looked like he belonged at the helm of a cruise ship. Although he looked too young to be a captain, didn't he? She chided herself for even asking such a question and didn't know what to say to this handsome stranger.

Thankfully, he just held out his hand for her to shake. "My name is Nicholas Becket, but most of my friends call me Nick." There was that smile again.

She shook hands with him and returned his friendly smile. When his hand grasped hers, a surge of desire unlike any other she had experienced before rushed through her.

He went on. "What kind of job are you looking for?"

"I am hoping to work as the boutique manager," she said. Finally, she was speaking in full sentences again. "I have a lot of experience with that sort of work. I was just interviewed by the recruitment administrator Monique Chadwick, and I think it went pretty well." Wait, what? She had a good feeling about the interview but to tell a total stranger it went well sounded bold.

He turned his smile on her again. "Well, I wish you the best of luck, Lily, and I hope to see you aboard the Moonlight Queen. It is going to be a fantastic vessel. Would you like a cup of coffee? I was just heading over to the refreshment room to get one. It has already been a very long day for me."

"Sure," she said. What was she doing now? First, she came to this crazy interview, and now she had agreed to have coffee with a complete stranger? Even if he was a gorgeous man in uniform, the entire scenario was very out of character for her. She ignored the monologue inside her head and smiled up at Nick. "Lead the way."

They headed out of the conference room and into a lounge. A station had been set up with coffee and pastries. The sights and smell of the extensive array of foods laid out on the table made her stomach rumble, but she was too nervous to eat, so she fixed herself a coffee. She continued to study him as they took a seat at one of the tables. He was lean but also muscular, and she couldn't help but notice he didn't wear a wedding ring. Nick stirred his coffee and looked over at her. His scorching gaze almost melted her on the spot.

"So Lily, why do you want to work on a cruise ship?"

She loved the way her name sounded in his cool, sexy voice. He had a small scar on his right cheek, which she noticed while trying to avoid the intense gaze of his brilliant eyes. She attempted to sound as interesting as possible as she formulated her answer.

"Well, I'm looking for a change of pace and scenery. This job would give me both of those things. Besides, it looks fun and exciting to work on a cruise ship. Is it?" She sat back and tasted her coffee, but she barely registered the fragrant brew since he dominated all of her senses.

He looked at her with his stunning blue eyes. "Yes and no. There are fun times, but it is a lot of hard work. I've had my share of both. It can be exciting, yes. But you must be dedicated to the job first and foremost. Do you think you are up for the challenge?"

Lily smiled a nervous smile. She was being interviewed again and she didn't like it, despite the fact that this handsome man in uniform was asking the questions. "Yes, of course." She was using a much more confident tone than she was actually feeling and she surprised herself, for the second time today. "I have a lot of experience, and I'm no stranger to hard work." There, she had told him. Then, he smiled at her again and her stomach dropped.

"Good to know. We are always looking for dedicated employees to join the Caribbean Paradise family. Do you live here, near Cape Canaveral?"

"Actually, I live in Orchard Park. But it is not too far away, just over an hour drive from here. Where do you live?"

"On a cruise ship most of the time. But I do have a condo in St. Petersburg, where the corporate headquarters are located." He glanced at his watch and then frowned. "Well, I would love to keep chatting with you, Lily, but I must get back to my interviews now."

"Of course." Lily stood and prepared to leave. She didn't want to keep him from his work, but she had to admit, she was a little bit disappointed their conversation had been cut short. There was so much more she wanted to know about this man, but it just wasn't meant to be. "Thank you so much for your time. It was a pleasure to meet you." She held out her hand for him to shake.

Instead, he grasped her hand and brought it to his lips. His kiss was so delicate, she almost fainted on the spot. The touch of his skin on hers was warm, light, and inviting. She imagined how his lips would feel on the rest of her body. What was going on with her? Was she losing the tenuous grip she had on her sanity?

"No, Lily," he said. "The pleasure was all mine." He paused for a moment. "Would you like to have dinner with me tonight? Unless of course you have other plans and have to head back home."

Lily hesitated. She had been on a few casual dates since her divorce six months earlier, but she had never been asked out by a complete stranger. Sympathetic friends, just trying to help her get on with her life, set up most of the one-date-only events she had attended. But none of the nice yet ordinary men made her feel the way she did right now.

Electricity crackled between them. She was certain they had a strong, unexplained connection even if her rational side was telling her it wasn't a smart idea to get involved with this guy. Despite her misgivings, she found her voice. "No, I don't have to get back home, so yes, I would like to have dinner with you, Captain Becket." There. She had overruled her common sense yet again, and went with her gut. A warm flush crawled across her face again, but she just didn't care. This was what she wanted, and she was going for it. There was no turning back now.

"Wonderful," he said. "I'll meet you in the hotel lounge, say six o'clock?"

"Yes." She smiled and hoped she didn't sound too nervous. "See you then." He let her hand go, and they parted ways. Lily walked toward the lobby with a grin on her face and the feel of Nick's lips on her hand still etched in her mind.

****

Nick walked back down the hall, thinking about the beautiful girl he had just met. She was pretty and friendly, but she had a look in her exquisite emerald eyes that he couldn't quite read. He wanted to know more about her and hear her story. His charming ways had worked again when he had asked her to dinner.

Lily wasn't like most of the girls he often dated, though. She had a depth to her he just couldn't put his finger on. This was not a quality he normally admired in women. Nevertheless, he found himself wishing he could take her in his arms again, like he had earlier when she fell into him. There was a definite attraction growing between them. He would make sure she got the job she wanted. Being a Becket did have its advantages.

He could lose himself forever in those luscious scarlet lips. And he could imagine running his hands through her honey-colored hair, which fell in soft waves past her shoulders to mid-back. She was tall, about five-foot-eight, he guessed, but at six-foot-two, he towered over her. She had been dressed conservatively in a gray tailored suit with a blazer and a white shirt. But he could tell that underneath all that professional façade was a sexy trim figure. These thoughts made him stop dead in his tracks. Was he falling for this girl he'd just met? That wasn't his usual style. He was used to women gushing all over him, and his countless one-night-stands were proof he was not a one-woman man. *Pull yourself together, it's just dinner.*

He was indeed the captain of the ship, and as the eldest son in his family, he was also the sole heir to the Caribbean Paradise fortune. All of the ships in the vast enterprise had been in the Becket family for three generations, and he would inherit it all one day. But the money and prestige just didn't mean a whole lot to him. He was more about living in the moment and although he had made a promise to his family, he doubted having dinner with an exquisite woman would break his new rule. At least not too much.

In fact, his father had been urging him in recent months, to stop sailing around searching for paradise and come to work in the corporate offices in St. Petersburg. Robert Becket wanted Nick to learn about the business side of the company. Nick, however, wasn't ready for that level of responsibility. The new ship was calling to him, and he couldn't resist sailing the brand new Moonlight Queen at least for a while before he settled down.

Despite this, he promised his father he would get more involved, to help more with the corporate side of the business. He had started by volunteering to hire officers at the job fair. He loathed this type of work, but running into Ms. Lily Kingston had been a welcome diversion to this dreaded day.

When Lily was out of sight, Nick pulled her resume out of his pocket. In the chaos of bumping into each other, he had been able to take it without her noticing. Glancing at it, he was pleased to see it contained all her personal information such as her address and phone number. He put it back in his pocket and set off to find his friend Monique Chadwick to ask her about Lily's interview.

He was wasting time; he had his own interviews to do. But as usual, what he wanted came first and work could wait. He made a mental note not to keep Lily Kingston waiting, though. He was pretty sure he didn't want her to be the one that got away.

Nick spotted Monique across the room, just finishing up an interview. She was a professional woman in her mid-fifties, dressed in a tailored navy pant suit.

Once the interviewee had left the table, he sauntered over and sat down.

She looked up at him. "Hi, Nick," she said and smiled. "How are the interviews going today?"

"Hey, Monique. Good to see you again. Everything is going well. Say, did you interview a woman named Lily Kingston this morning?"

She shuffled through the files on her table, searching for Lily's name. Monique stopped at one of her first interview packages and smiled up at Nick.

"Yes I did."

"What can you tell me about her?" He tried not to sound too eager for information, but Lily had intrigued him from the moment he laid eyes on her.

Monique leafed through her papers and then settled on the notes she had taken. "Well, I think she would be a very dedicated employee, and she has quite a bit of experience in the retail sector. Before moving to Florida, she worked as a manager for the Waterford chain of department stores in Michigan. Right now, she is working as a receptionist at the Orchard Park Insurance Company. Customer service is a big part of her job. I was impressed with her credentials, Nick, but we do have a lot of other applicants for the boutique manager's position."

"Yes, I know," he said and turned on his megawatt grin. "But I think she might be the best candidate for the job, wouldn't you say?" He held his breath, waiting for Monique to answer him.

"I think she would be a good fit, and you're the boss, so if you want her, she's all yours."

Nick smiled at her comment. Yes, Lily could be all his. Then he refocused his thoughts. "Thanks, Monique. You're the best. Oh, and can we keep this conversation just between us?" He didn't want Lily to know he was meddling in her life on the very day they met. She came across to him as a proud woman who might not take interference too well. It wasn't worth the risk.

"Sure, Nick, no problem. Does this mean we can cancel all the other interviews for this position?"

"Yes, I think so. I know Lily is the best candidate. Best not to waste the other applicants' time. Maybe you could find them some other positions if they are still interested?" He had no proof whatsoever he was right, but when Nicholas Becket wanted something, he made sure he got it. "See you later, Monique. And thanks again."

"Yes. Will do. See you..." She was already looking down and leafing through other notes, getting ready for her next interview. Nick strode away, pleased with himself. When he looked down at his watch, he swore under his breath. He was late again, and he had wanted to keep this day on track. However, he was certain Lily was worth the craziness of the next few hours, which he would spend rushing through interviews in order to get caught up.

****

A smile grew on Lily's face as she walked through the spacious lobby. This day had turned out almost perfect. She was happier than she had been in months, and she couldn't believe she was having dinner with Nick, the captain of the Moonlight Queen, no less. She flashed back to an image of his stunning eyes and sexy smile. It made her pulse quicken and an intense heat radiate through her body.

What would it be like to date a man like him? As soon as that question came to mind, she dismissed it. With a smile like that, she would be surprised if he didn't have a girlfriend, or one in every port. They had just met today and chatted for a few moments. She reasoned he was just being friendly by inviting her to dinner. He didn't want to date her. Besides, she wasn't sure if she was over the horrible break-up with her ex-husband.

Since she had the afternoon free before she had to meet Nick, she wanted to treat herself to a long walk in and around Cape Canaveral. It was just a short drive away, and she could see the ships from there. Lily could get a feel for the city that housed the world famous port, where dozens of cruise ships sailed away to paradise every day.

She headed toward the exit and out the front doors to where her car was parked. As she took a short drive up the port, Lily remembered the last time she had been to the Cape. It had been a few years earlier with her ex-husband Derek. They had taken a romantic three-day cruise to the Bahamas. If someone had told her five years ago she would end up a divorcee and working as a receptionist, she would have laughed at them. Her idea of a fabulous life had not included ordering pens and paper clips for a living. Oh, the plans she had dreamed of for her and Derek.

She tried to put those thoughts out of her mind. Everything was about to change, she hoped. She had arrived at her destination, parked the car, and walked around the terminal. The day was beautiful with the sunlight shining down on her and a gentle breeze coming off the water. Lily was peaceful and calm amongst the hustle and bustle of passengers coming and going.

The ships looked magnificent harbored in the port. They were very majestic. One ship in particular caught her eye with its white balconies stretching for miles and the hull painted black in sharp contrast. Intricate designs graced the bow, then she noticed the familiar Caribbean Paradise logo emblazoned on the side. This ship was the Sunlight King. It was larger than life from her point of view. Lily stood in awe of the sight that made her want the job more than ever, so she could hop aboard one of these giants and explore every deck.

She then took another drive down to Cocoa Village and spent the afternoon there. It was a quaint little town just a short drive from Cape Canaveral. There she stopped at a local deli for lunch. A whimsical little place that served soup, sandwiches, and salads. She could smell the fresh baking bread as she approached the entrance. They had wonderful looking turkey croissant sandwiches, and she ordered one with a glass of iced tea. After the nice young girl at the counter put her order together, Lily took it outside. She took a seat on the patio and marveled at how much her life was changing in such a short time.

She reflected back and told herself she had been more than prepared. She had polished her resume, organized her other documents the night before, and made sure she looked very professional for her interview. Lily had explained the duties of her current job at the insurance company to the recruitment administrator and emphasized how she was a perfect fit with what the cruise line was looking for. Finally, she had described how flexible her current lifestyle was without getting into the details of her divorce.

Lily was pleased with herself and believed she had done well, despite her nerves. The interviewer had pointed out what her job would entail. She also mentioned they would be conducting interviews all day, and if she was selected for the position she would be contacted by phone. Lily had thanked her for her time and then it was over. This could be the opportunity of a lifetime.

Uninvited, doubt set in. Was she too old for a change like this? *Stop it, right now.* Her inner voice always put her down, so she tried to ignore it. Instead, she focused on the wealth of job knowledge she had gathered over the years in order to make her a good candidate for the position. Besides, her young competitors couldn't possibly have the over ten years of work experience she had.

She finished her lunch, then spent the afternoon walking around the town and browsing at the local shops. Wanting to impress Nick, she bought a new dress for dinner and even treated herself to a pretty silver bracelet at one of the local jewelers. She got it to symbolize the beginning of the new life she was building. *If* she got the job that is, but she was feeling more optimistic than ever that she was headed down a new and exciting path.

The afternoon melted away as she enjoyed the village and all it had to offer. When she looked at her watch a couple of hours later, she saw that her sightseeing would have to end. She had to head back soon to meet Nick for dinner.

Nick. Would he be a part of the new life she was trying to build? She couldn't be sure, but there was only one way to find out.

****

Nick hurried through the rest of his afternoon, distracted by thoughts of Lily. When his last interview was over, he headed back up to his hotel suite for a quick shower, shave, and change of clothes before he met her for dinner.

Lily. He loved the way her name sounded on his lips, and thinking about her soft curves and long legs made him rigid with desire.

He wasn't entirely sure what he was doing with

her. She wasn't like any girl he had ever met before. One thing he did know was he wanted to get to know her inside and out. Man, he was beginning to lose his cool over this woman.

Nick noticed the redhead from the night before had left a note for him on the bedside table with her name and phone number on it. He crumpled it up and threw it in the garbage. Then he called down to the front desk to make a reservation at the steakhouse restaurant in the hotel. He had been there many times. The place was quiet and intimate. They had an extensive menu, and the food was superb.

The maid had been in to straighten the room so the space was neat and tidy. He was leaving to go back home to St. Petersburg tomorrow, so he figured he could pack up some of his stuff, just in case Lily came back to his room. He was hopeful, but he was pretty sure she wasn't that kind of girl.

He took a quick glance in the mirror before heading downstairs. Dressed in a black suit and tie with a white shirt, he looked polished and refined. People often told him he resembled a model more than a ship's captain, but he scoffed at that notion. At six-foot-two, he was a tall, striking figure. His blond hair gleamed from his recent shower, and his blue eyes shined with excitement. Once everything was in order, he headed downstairs.

Nick got to the lounge a few minutes before his six o'clock date. While he waited for Lily, he ordered a beer and looked around the impressive space. The restaurant was decorated in earth tones with a rich walnut bar in the center of the room. As he sat down, his nerves had him on edge. He couldn't remember a time when a woman had made him this jumpy. He took a swig of his beer and told himself to relax.

Just then, he saw her across the room. She was walking toward him in a sleeveless silver dress. It sparkled and hugged her curves in all the right places. She had piled her long hair on top of her head in a sexy twisted chignon. If she had makeup on, he couldn't tell. She was a natural beauty, but she looked more gorgeous than he remembered. He found himself craving her touch and sauntered over to meet her. When he gave her his million dollar smile, she returned it, and his hunger for her surged.

"Hello, Lily," he said in his deep smooth voice. He took her hand in his. Their touch created a spark that heightened his desire. "I'm glad you could make it. Would you like a drink?"

"Thank you for inviting me. I'm happy to be here and would love a glass of sangria if they have it."

"Coming right up. By the way, you look stunning tonight." He was surprised to discover his voice was full with unexpected emotion.

"Why, thank you, Captain. And you look very handsome as well."

He noticed her cheeks turn a light pink with his compliment, but it just added to her beauty. "Please," he said as he still held onto her hand. "Let's sit down and relax."

Nick led her over to the bar and signaled the bartender. He ordered for her and then motioned toward a stool, before he reluctantly let her hand go and took the seat next to her. "How was your afternoon? I hope you didn't get bored." He tried to keep the conversation light, even though all he wanted to do was reach out and caress her bare shoulder.

The bartender came back and placed their drinks in front of them. Then he discreetly sauntered away.

"It was great, thanks for asking. I did a little sightseeing and some shopping. How about you?"

"It was okay. Interviews aren't really my thing. I much prefer to be out on the open water commanding the ship. But unfortunately, I think my days as a captain are coming to an end."

"Why? I can tell you are passionate about your career. What would make you give it up?"

Nick hesitated. He wasn't used to revealing so much about himself and his family to the women he dated. Instead of opening up to her, which he strangely wanted to do, he delayed her questions. "I promise I'll tell you the whole story over dinner. Which reminds me, do you like steak?"

"I love it."

"Wonderful."

He was relieved he had chosen a restaurant she liked. They finished their drinks at the bar and headed over to the other side of the hotel where the restaurant was located.

It was dark and intimate where they were seated in a quiet booth inside the Portside Steakhouse. Lily marveled to Nick about the nautical style of the space with its cozy tables and walls decorated with tasteful seaside ornaments. The tension seeped from Nick's neck and shoulders as he sipped the vintage red wine he had ordered for them. Lily sat across from him and looked as if she was enjoying herself as well.

They perused the menu, taking their time and enjoying each other's company. They both ordered steak for dinner, he the top sirloin and she the filet mignon. Each was served with a baked potato and seasonal vegetables. They also had some fresh baked bread with their wine.

Nick found himself beginning to trust this charming and graceful lady. She had a genuine quality about her and was interested in hearing about his life and family. The alarming thing to him was that he responded to her questions in an open and honest manner. He couldn't remember a time when he had ever acted that way with a woman.

Lily brought the subject of his family up again while they were eating. She looked at him with an intense emerald stare. "Well, Captain Becket, you promised me an explanation as to why you're sailing days are numbered. Time to fess up."

"Okay," he said as he smiled at her direct approach. "The truth is my father, who is the chief owner and operator of the company, isn't well. He is older, but has always been very vibrant and the lifeblood of Caribbean Paradise. But about three months ago, he was diagnosed with lung cancer. The kicker is he's never smoked a day in his life. He is going through some treatments, but we aren't sure how effective they will be. Anyway, my two brothers and sister already work at headquarters, but they need my help." He sighed. Relief flooded his system after his confession. Being able to talk about it somehow lessened his burden. He looked across the table, and her angelic face was full of empathy.

"Oh, Nick, I'm so sorry. You sure have a lot going on. And I can tell your family is very important to you."

"Yes, they are," he replied. He was now

uncomfortable with his heartfelt confession and attempted to turn the conversation in another direction. "Well, enough about me and my problems. How about ordering dessert?"

"Sure," she said. He appreciated that she went along with his abrupt change of subject.

"I love anything chocolate."

They lingered, sharing a mocha flavored mousse and the rest of the wine. Lily told Nick about her fascination with the cruise ships at the terminal this afternoon. Nick glanced down at his watch. "If you loved that, you have to see the view of the ships at sunset from my balcony. C'mon." He signaled the waiter and charged the dinner to his room. Then he reached for Lily's hand.

"Nick, wait," she said. "I think it's time for me to be heading home. Besides, I'm not so sure I should be going to your room. After all, we just met today."

"Oh. I'm sorry for asking, that was very presumptuous of me. I just know how much you love the ships, and there is no better time to see them than right now. If it makes you feel uncomfortable, maybe another time? But do you have to go so soon? We could go for a walk instead?" Nick wanted, no needed, to spend more time with Lily and get to know her better.

"No," she said and looked up at him.

His stomach clenched. His charming ways hadn't worked this time, and he wasn't quite sure what to do or say. But this time it was Lily who made the first move. She took a deep breath before she spoke again.

"Let's go see this beautiful view. I hope it's as gorgeous as you say it is."

He could hardly believe it, but he managed to keep

his composure. "Great. I promise you won't be disappointed." He made a vow not to take it too far with her. He didn't want to frighten her away. But that notion faded into the background as he took her delicate hand in his large one and led her to the elevator.

Nick was staying in the penthouse suite. Lily gushed to him about the space with its classy clean lines, modern decor done in soft shades of white, and spacious sitting room. Nick rushed her through there and into the bedroom, though.

"Nick…" Lily protested.

He just grinned at her. "Hurry up, the balcony is through here. I don't want you to miss it."

He threw open the French doors, and they stepped out onto the large outdoor space. He could see from her expression that Lily was captivated by the ships in the distance and the dazzling red-orange of the setting sun. It filled the sky and sparkled on the ocean.

At this distance and height, it gave them a clear view of the entire port. Many vessels were docked in the harbor. The ships looked like miniature versions of themselves and were twinkling with an infinite number of lights. Nick quietly studied a speechless Lily for several minutes. When she took her eyes off the seascape and looked at him, he saw wonder and awe in her face.

"Oh, Nick," she said, almost breathless. "This is one of the most beautiful views I have ever seen."

Seeing her there with the last of the sunlight glittering on her hair and that dreamy look in her eye made his longing rise. If he couldn't have her, Nick would shatter into a million pieces. "Not half as beautiful as you look right now," he rasped. His self-control was hanging on by a thread.

He couldn't stop himself as he wrapped his strong arms around her, feeling the warmth radiate off her body. Her breasts were pressed against his chest, and he ached with the need to peel off her clothes. He kissed her with tenderness at first and then with more depth as their tongues intertwined. The wine and chocolate in her kiss was a heady combination. They stood together like that for the longest time, before Nick forced himself to break away.

"Lily. I want you. Here and now, like no woman I have ever wanted. But if you're not ready, tell me. We can stop right now. Just know, if I kiss you again, I'm not going to be able to control myself." He waited a long moment for her answer.

"I want you too, Nick." Her voice sounded like the soft caressing breeze that surrounded them. "Don't stop—"

Covering her mouth, he silenced her with a crushing kiss. She had said the words he had wanted to hear, and he wasn't going to let her change her mind.

He swept her off her feet to carry her into the bedroom. She was feather light in his embrace with her arms around his neck and her body pressed against him. The cool white walls of the room and the satin bedspread were in sharp contrast to the heat they were creating.

He set her down on the bed and slipped off her high-heeled sandals. He kissed his way up her calf to the creamy flesh of her thigh and lingered there, filling his nostrils with the delicate scent of her perfume. The notes of coconut and hibiscus were intoxicating.

She leaned over and tugged at his jacket, spurring

him to discard it and his tie in a heap on the floor. The buttons on his shirt came undone one by one under her silky fingertips to reveal his torso and a large tattoo of an anchor with a ship's wheel on his chest. A rope encircled the design. Lily traced the image with her delicate touch and kissed it before working her way down his chest to his abs. The feel of her lips on him was driving him to the edge.

Nick reached down and grasped her again. He pulled her up so that his lips met hers in another blaze of passion, while he reached around and unzipped her dress. Then he peeled it off her, revealing a pink lace bra and bikini panties. *God, she is gorgeous.* Her blonde tresses cascaded down her back as he pulled the pins one by one from her hair. He stroked the long strands with one hand, and they were as soft as silk.

She pushed his shirt off his shoulders and went to work releasing the button on his pants. His groin was tight, straining with need for her. She freed him from his slacks and boxers and took him in her hands. As she stroked the length of him he shuddered with ecstasy. He wasn't going to last much longer.

He undid her bra, kissed her perfect breasts, and dragged a moan of pleasure from her as he slid his hands down her body. Then her legs parted, inviting him into her. He entered her, slow and tentative at first, but she was ready for him. When she wrapped her legs around his waist he increased the tempo, and she matched it, whispering his name. His slim hips moved, thrusting in and out of her. Just before he truly lost his mind, they came together in an earth-shattering climax. They became one on the deepest level two people could achieve.

Afterward, they lay in each other's arms. Nick was spent but peaceful and happy.

He broke the easy silence that had settled around them. "Lily, how are you? Are you okay?"

"Yes," she said and yawned. "Just tired, let's sleep now…"

"Sure," he said and wrapped his strong arms around her small frame. He settled back down on the pillow with her body, so soft and warm, pressed to his side.

As Nick drifted off to sleep with Lily in his arms, he was content. More content, in fact, than he had been in a very long time.

****

Lily awoke several hours later, tired and confused as she struggled to open her eyes. Sleep was trying to overtake again her, but she fought against it. Where was she? Not in her bed in Orchard Park, that was for sure. She could hear soft breathing beside her, and her eyes flew open. Nick. He was sleeping peacefully on his side facing her. He looked young and vulnerable, not the confident captain she had met at the job fair. Her stomach dropped as she remembered what had happened between them just a few hours ago.

Panic rose, and she shook her head to try to clear the last of the sleep from her foggy brain. No, she wasn't ready for this. What had she been thinking? *More like not thinking. How could I let this happen?* She had made a promise to herself that she wouldn't let herself get hurt again, and yet, here she was having a one-night-stand with a man she barely knew. They hadn't even used protection. Though, that was the least of her worries right now. The whole evening had been a recipe for disaster if there ever was one. She had to get out of there. Now.

Not making a sound, she slipped out of bed, collected her clothes that were strewn about the floor, and dressed as fast as she could. She grabbed her purse on the way to the door. Just before she opened it, she had an idea. Lily had to end this, for good. She took the pen and paper from the nightstand and scrawled a one-line note. Then she folded it and placed it on the table where he couldn't miss it.

She glanced back at him for the last time. He was so handsome, and she had experienced a wonderful evening with him, but it wouldn't work. Lily couldn't stop herself as she ran for the door and out into the hallway. She had to put as much distance between her and Nick as she could. Maybe then her panic would subside, but there were no guarantees of that either.

Chapter Two

"You did what?" exclaimed Victoria. As Lily's best friend, she had a flair for the dramatic, but she couldn't have found a friend who cared more about her. On Sunday, when Lily had returned from Cape Canaveral, she finally worked up the courage to call her. She wanted to tell her what was going on even though she hadn't figured it all out herself. Lily wanted the job on the cruise ship with a passion, despite what had transpired with Nick.

"I know it sounds crazy, but I really feel like I need a change in my life right now. The ship is gorgeous, and the people at the interview were nice. And you know how much I hate my job at the insurance company. I'm so frustrated, some days I think I might just go in there and quit on the spot. Anyway, who knows what's going to happen."

Lily continued without waiting for a reply. "There were a lot of people at the job fair, and I'm not sure how many people they are hiring." Then she stopped, not sure if she should mention Nick. Lily needed to sort through her thoughts first, but she also wanted to talk to someone, so she found herself unable to stop her runaway words. "Oh, and I ran into the captain of the ship, Nicholas Becket, and he asked me out to dinner."

"Did you go?"

"Yes, and I slept with him too." *I've gone this far. I*

may as well confess to everything.

Victoria let out a long sigh on the other end of the line. "Lily, why would you do such a thing? You are indeed one of the most beautiful people I know, so I'm not surprised you were asked out. But this whole sleeping with a stranger is totally out of character for you."

"Well, it just kind of happened. He was so tall, good-looking, and easy to talk to. I think I just got caught up in the moment, but I realize now it was all a big mistake. I still want the job, but I don't think I should see Nick again."

"You know how much I love you and want you to be happy." This was true. "I feel like you are running away from your problems, not dealing with them. Besides if you leave town, what would I do without you?"

"I don't even know if I will get the job. As far as Nick is concerned, it's over. I'm not running away, but I think I just might need a change of scenery for a while. Derek and all his baggage is now in the past. I need to start a new chapter in my life. You know I would come and visit you all the time. Besides, you are so busy with work, Tom, and the twins, you won't even realize I'm gone."

Lily adored Victoria's husband Tom and their four-year old twins Jake and Liam. She tried to spend as much time with them as possible. Of course, she had more than enough time on her hands since the divorce, and they had grown closer than ever.

Victoria had been a rock for her during the past year. Despite her crazy schedule, she always made time for Lily. Whether she needed a shoulder to cry on or just a sympathetic ear, her best friend was there. And she would miss her, but she had to do this, despite what had happened with Nick.

"I'm just going to wait and see what happens." She hoped her evening with Nick hadn't ruined her chances. Only time would tell.

"Okay, I won't go into full panic mode yet! But keep me posted if anything changes."

Lily promised she would, and the conversation drifted toward work, the twins, and other things going on in their lives.

After her phone call, Lily collapsed on her sofa. An image of Nick drifted through her mind when she reflected back on last night. Despite the fact that Nick was uneasy about personal conversations, he had opened up to her. And when he had abruptly changed the subject, she had gone along with it. She had tried to hide her shock when he revealed that his family owned the entire cruise line. Although truth be told, money couldn't buy happiness; it was never more evident than in Nick's story.

Lily didn't like the way she had left things with Nick, but it was for the best. Not only had she never had a one-night stand, she also had never snuck out of a hotel room at four in the morning. When she awoke in Nick's bed, she was overcome with fear. Fear that she had made another mistake. Even though she had told Victoria that Derek was in the past, she just wasn't ready to move forward. Her ex-husband had wounded her on the deepest level possible, and although she was beginning to heal, she just couldn't let herself take that risk again.

****

Nick awoke late Sunday, but today he didn't have anywhere to be. He smiled and reached for Lily but found the bed empty and cold. He opened his eyes to sunlight streaming in, illuminating the room. He rose in an instant and did a search of the entire suite. She was gone.

Nick was hollow inside. He raked his hands through his hair and walked toward the balcony doors to get some fresh air. It was then he noticed the white folded piece of paper on the desk. Picking it up, he made his way out onto the balcony. He took a deep breath but couldn't seem to get enough oxygen. What happened? He gulped in the fresh ocean breeze and with a shaking hand opened the note. It read:

Dear Nick,

I'm sorry...I think I have made a terrible mistake. Please don't try to contact me.

Lily

His worst fear had come true. Nick had pushed her too far, too fast, and now she was gone. He should just move on like he had countless times before with numerous other women. Yet something about Lily was different. He had opened up to her, bared his true emotions instead of the superficial talk and smooth pick-up lines he used with other women. Not to mention the passion filled romance they had shared last night. He needed to see her again, but she clearly didn't want to see him. What was he going to do now?

****

On Monday, Nick was back in St. Petersburg with Colin. The two brothers had pre-arranged this dinner to talk about the business. Nick just blurted out the story about Lily without thinking it through. Nick got a boatload of unsolicited advice, and he didn't like what his brother had to say.

"Geez, will you just forget about her? Sure, she sounds a bit classier than what you are used to, but so what? You'll find another one just around the corner, now drink up big brother." Colin leaned back as he finished speaking and took a swig of his beer.

"Yeah, you're probably right," Nick said with a casual tone he did not feel. He couldn't stop thinking about Lily during his waking hours. Images of their bodies melding together haunted his dreams.

Nick suspected telling his younger brother about Lily might have been a bad idea, and judging by Colin's cavalier attitude his doubt was confirmed. Nevertheless, he was desperate to talk to someone. They were as close as brothers could be, despite the six years between them. At thirty-five Nick was supposed to be the wise older brother, but he didn't often feel or act this way. Today was no exception.

"Well, enough about me," Nick said. "How is Dad doing?"

"He's hanging in there, but this whole cancer thing has been hard on him and Mom. We still don't know the prognosis at this point. There's another round of chemotherapy coming up for him next week."

"Oh." A pang of guilt washed through Nick for not being there for his parents and helping out more. But he had this hardwired instinct to be out on the open water and wasn't sure how to curb the urge. He would settle down, someday. He just didn't have a strict timeline.

He pulled himself away from his conscience and asked, "What's new with you?"

"Life is good," Colin said and smiled the same

winning smile all the Becket men possessed. He ran a hand through his dark brown hair, which was in sharp contrast to Nick's blond locks, but they had the same devastating blue eyes. "Work is busy, but I'm managing…especially with the help of the gorgeous new assistant I just hired. She's smart and smoking hot, who could ask for more? Hey, I could see if she has a friend for you. Any idea when you're going to join us at headquarters?"

"Not quite yet. I know Dad needs me, but I want to command the new ship for a while." He had been even more enthusiastic about the prospect when he imagined working with Lily on-board. But wait. What had Colin just said? Nick had almost missed it. He suddenly knew what he had to do to win Lily back, and he had important work to do. There wasn't a moment to waste.

****

The next week flew by in a blur for Lily. Marguerite, her boss, had gotten a terrible case of the flu, so she hadn't been to work all week. This suited Lily just fine. She ran the office like the capable receptionist she was.

With no word from the cruise line, she wondered if she would ever hear from them. After a few more days without a phone call, she figured they must have chosen someone else for the position. It was disappointing of course, but since life hadn't been going her way for quite some time, not too surprising.

Her optimistic attitude had lasted for one glorious day. The day of the interview and her evening with Nick had been magical, but now she was back to her old self. A little depressed and somewhat bored, but it was what she was used to. Besides, Nick must have made sure she didn't get the job after she ran out on him in the middle of the night. All in all, it was for the best.

On Friday as she was about to close the office for the weekend, her phone rang. "Good afternoon, Orchard Park Insurance Company, Lily Kingston speaking. How may I help you?"

"Hello, Lily." She recognized his deep masculine voice at once. "It's Nicholas Becket calling from the Caribbean Paradise Cruise Line."

"Nick," she said. His smooth voice made her nervous, but she was thrilled to hear from him despite the fact warning bells rang in her rational mind. With a somewhat shaky conviction she continued. "I asked you not to contact me."

"This is strictly business. I promise you," he replied. "I took the liberty of retrieving your file from the recruitment administrator Monique Chadwick. I have to say I'm very impressed with your credentials. Our team would be lucky to have someone with your excellent qualities working for us. I'm calling on behalf of Caribbean Paradise to offer you the position of boutique manager aboard the Moonlight Queen."

Lily was stunned. She paused for a minute to catch her breath.

"Lily, are you still there?"

"Yes," she stammered. "Sorry, yes, thank you…" She'd love to have the job, but she wasn't sure it was worth the risk of getting tangled up with Nick again. She took a deep breath. "As much as I want to accept your offer, I'm not sure it's a good idea for us to see each other again."

"Lily, I'm not going to be on the ship, I'm working

33

in the corporate office now." There was a tone she couldn't quite read in his voice. "You are the perfect choice for this position. Please don't turn it down because of me."

She wanted this chance at a new life, and Nick sounded sincere. She'd be a fool to give up this good fortune. She regained some of her composure. "Yes, thank you. I would like to accept the position."

"Great. A representative from the cruise ship will be calling you in the next few days to give you all the information you need. The ship sails on the Saturday before Labor Day. You will need to start about a week earlier to work at getting the shop ready for the passengers. Do you have any questions?"

"No, not right now." She couldn't even think straight, let alone come up with any questions that made sense. "But I'm sure I can ask the representative if something comes up." She hoped she sounded at least halfway intelligent. "And, Nick...thank you for understanding."

"Sure thing, Lily," he said. "Well, on behalf of Caribbean Paradise, I would like to welcome you to our family."

"Thank you again. I am very excited and think this will be a great opportunity." She noticed her voice was filled with an unfamiliar quality. And then she recognized it, hope.

Nick said good-bye and hung up. Lily got up from her desk and let out a cry of joy. She couldn't believe she had gotten the job. She was going to work on a cruise ship! Hearing Nick's voice again had unnerved her somewhat, but she was relieved that he had moved on. And being a true gentleman, he didn't hold a grudge. She would have to send him a heartfelt letter to the corporate headquarters to thank him.

Lily couldn't contain her joy and excitement. There was so much to do in order to get ready for this new phase of her life. She pulled a piece of paper out of her drawer, grabbed a pen, and wrote her letter of resignation to the Orchard Park Insurance Company.

****

Nick blew out a big sigh as he hung up the phone. He had done it. Memories surfaced of their perfect night not long ago, the dinner, the intimate conversation, and the night of pure passion. His primal need for her rose up within him. He would win her back soon enough. He just had to take it one step at a time.

He hated lying to her as he was indeed going to be commanding the Moonlight Queen, but he couldn't take the risk of telling her, for fear she would turn down the job. Once she figured out what he had done, he hoped it would be too late for her to back out. The Becket men always got what they wanted, and he wanted Lily, badly. Now for the next phase of his plan.

****

The weeks flew by, and suddenly the end of August had arrived. Lily was in her apartment packing up the last of her belongings. She would board the cruise ship the following morning and start her new career. Two weeks ago, she had given notice on her rented studio apartment and had quit her job at the insurance company. Her furniture and the belongings she didn't need were packed and placed in a storage unit

Lily looked around her small apartment. Although she had lived here for the past six months, it had never been home. When she had married Derek five years ago, they had bought a beautiful three-bedroom bungalow. It had been sold off during the divorce proceedings. He had broken her heart when he ran off and left her for his much younger assistant.

This happened after she had given up a promising career as a store manager in Michigan and moved to Florida with him. He was starting his own personal injury law firm. She had supported him by getting the job at the insurance company and put up with his long hours and hefty student loans. Since her parents had died when she was in her early twenties, she had no extended family to speak of, but this was all becoming a distant memory now. It seemed a lifetime ago that she was a happily married woman. Now, she was ready to move on to the new future she was building in paradise.

Lily had shared a tearful dinner with Victoria and her husband Tom the night before. She would miss them of course, but she promised to visit when she could. In the end, Victoria had conceded this was a good move for her, just like all best friends should do. She had wished her good luck and made her promise to keep in touch.

Now, all she had left to do was pack up the last of her things she was taking with her and get on the bus bound for Cape Canaveral the following morning. The cruise ship company had offered her a one-year contract with the option to renew each year if they were satisfied with her work. It had taken her weeks to gather the necessary forms and documents that were needed to secure her employment. The makeshift plan that she had conjured up just a short time ago was all coming together. She couldn't remember when she had been happier. Well, of course she had been happy with Derek, but this was different. Lily was ready to do something for herself. As she drifted off to sleep the night before the beginning of her new life, she had dreams of beautiful beaches and magnificent sunsets. And as if her subconscious was trying to tell her something, a gorgeous ship captain to share them with.

The next morning when she woke up, it was hazy and drizzling rain. Not even the dismal weather could dampen her spirits. She had checked in with the cruise line and calculated what time she would arrive at Port Canaveral to board the ship. As she dressed in cropped khaki pants and a blue T-shirt, she grabbed a light sweater in case the bus was air-conditioned. However, it had been so hot in Florida the past month she doubted if she would need it. Lily smiled at herself in the mirror as she brushed her hair and teeth. She put on a bit of mascara and blush, and then she was ready.

As she gathered up the last of her belongings, she looked around the small apartment. This was it. The start of a new chapter in her life. Then the doorbell rang. Who could that be? Victoria had to work today and besides, they had said their good-byes last night. The landlord had told her to put the keys in the mailbox after she locked up, and he would come by later to pick them up, so it wasn't him. The doorbell rang a second time.

Lily walked to the door and opened it. There stood Nick looking as handsome as ever. He was dressed in gray casual cargo shorts and a black short-sleeved polo shirt. His short blond hair was longer and spiked up. Gorgeous blue eyes shone as they searched hers. He looked incredible, and he was also wearing his devastating smile. Time stood still for her as she took in the sight of him.

"Hello, Lily," he said.

His voice was deep, sexy, and he was more beautiful than she remembered. She was weak in the knees at seeing him again. Shock and confusion surged through her with him standing on her doorstep. She had no idea what in the world to say to him.

"Hi," she managed. "What are you doing here?" That sounded a bit rude, but she had been so taken aback at the sight of him and before she could think straight, it was too late.

"Well, the cruise line sends a limousine for me, and I was coming right by your area, so I wanted to pick you up on the way. It's a pretty long bus ride, and you probably have a lot of stuff. My sister always packs half her closet for a weekend trip. I hoped you might enjoy traveling by car better, and we can get to know each other. After all, we are going to be working together for the next year."

"What?" she exclaimed. Now she was definitely being rude, but this was not what he had said on the phone.

"Look, Lily, I'm sorry if I misled you, but as it turns out, I will be commanding the Moonlight Queen after all, so why don't we try to get along, okay?"

She glared at him. "No, Nicholas Becket, it's not okay." She could feel heat rising up in her cheeks. "I wouldn't have accepted this job if there was a chance I would be seeing you again."

"Why? Am I ugly?"

He was trying to make light of the situation and diffuse some of her anger, but she wasn't buying it.

She stared at him. He was as far from ugly as anyone could get and she flashed back to their night of passion. His strong arms, his muscular abs and the feel of his lips all over her body. This was not helping. She shook her head to clear her thoughts and found her voice again.

"No, of course not, but I explained everything in the note I left for you."

His exquisite eyes narrowed at her. "No, you didn't. Saying sorry and you made a mistake is not an explanation, Lily Kingston. And although I'll admit, we may have taken things a little too fast, there is nothing wrong with two single people enjoying each other's company. And now, I want to get to know you better. I'll be on my best behavior, I promise. If not, you can tell the driver to dump me at the side of the road."

She couldn't help but smile. He did have a point. She hadn't told him her true feelings as to why she wasn't ready for a relationship, or even casual dating, if in fact that was what he had in mind. They didn't end up doing a lot of talking inside his suite. She did owe him an explanation, someday.

"Okay," she conceded. What harm could a chauffeured limousine ride do? They had spent so much time talking that she must have missed her bus by now. Then she remembered her manners. "Thank you. It's very generous of you to think of me. I actually do have a lot of stuff. Where are you coming from?"

"I was just visiting my family in St. Petersburg. Now we're headed straight to the Port. I'm sorry I didn't call first, but my cell phone battery died. Besides, I wanted to surprise you and see your reaction when you see the Moonlight Queen for the first time. She is magnificent. When I saw her last week, I was speechless. I also didn't want you to say no to me." He offered her a shy smile. This was the first time Lily had seen him express anything but pure confidence.

"Well, I can't start my new career by refusing the captain, now can I?" She was teasing him a little and even flirting! Lily was becoming a new woman and she liked the surge of confidence she was not only feeling, but also showing. But she reminded herself not to get carried away, again.

He smiled down at her. "No, you can't. Are you ready to go?"

"Yes, just about." She turned to stuff the last of her belongings in her suitcase. Then she looked up into his brilliant blue eyes and grinned. "I'm ready for my new life with Caribbean Paradise."

"Let's go." He picked up her suitcase and knapsack. "Paradise awaits."

She locked up her apartment for the very last time and followed Nick down the short flight of stairs to the ground floor. Then she gasped at the large elegant black vehicle and uniformed driver waiting for them at the curb. "Good morning, Ms. Kingston," the driver said as he opened the door for her. Nick helped her into the spacious back seat.

Lily caught a whiff of fresh brewed coffee. It smelled delicious, dark and smoky. She had missed having her morning coffee and breakfast. As if to remind her, her stomach rumbled in protest. There was a table set up in the limo with a carafe and some pastries. Nick slid into the seat across from her. "Please, help yourself to anything you want," he said.

"Great, thank you. I'm starving," Lily said and then

felt her cheeks flush with heat. Should she really be admitting to a man she hardly knew that she was so hungry? *Oh well, too late.*

"Good," he said. "There's lots to choose from. What would you like?"

"What I meant is, there was no leftover food in my fridge, so I was going to pick up something at the bus station."

"Trust me," Nick said and smiled his breathtaking smile. "This is better than anything you'd get at the bus station."

Lily just nodded and selected a cherry danish then poured herself a cup of the wonderful coffee before she sank into the soft leather seats and admired her surroundings. There was even a flat screen television and a sunroof. She hadn't ever been in a vehicle this elegant.

"If you like this, you'll love the cruise ship," he said.

She was indeed enjoying this and was excited to see Nick again, as much as she was trying to convince herself that she wasn't.

They chatted like old friends on the drive to Port Canaveral. He shared a bit about his past with her and she found it fascinating.

"I got my Bachelor's degree in Marine Engineering from Florida State University," he said. "Then I went on to my training with the United States Coast Guard. Those were pretty exciting times. I learned a lot. Once I graduated, I started on the cruise line and worked my way up from crew member to captain." At the age of thirty-five, this was quite an accomplishment.

"As the oldest son in my family, it was kind of

expected that I take over the business, one day. And I will, but not yet. I have such a love of the ocean. I was drawn to it. Still am. My parents understand and are supportive, but I sometimes feel like I'm letting them down."

He was doing it again. Nick was showing her his deepest thoughts and emotions. She smiled over at him.

"I'm sure they understand. After all, most parents' greatest wish is for their children to be happy."

Nick went on about his siblings, as if he couldn't help himself. He had two brothers, Colin and Jon, and he spoke with admiration about his older sister Grace, despite the fact she still teased him like he was a six-year-old.

"I'd like you to meet them one day. I promise we will call ahead first, not just show up at their front door."

She was a bit surprised at the comment but laughed at his joke. "I would love that. They sound very nice."

"They are, and I know they would like you. Now, enough about me. Tell me about you, Lily. Something we didn't cover in our first date."

Lily paused as she was unsure what to say to this beautiful gentleman. Her life was pretty boring compared to his, but she had to say something. There was a definite attraction growing between them, despite her constant denials. She didn't want to ruin it by telling him about her bad luck in recent years. Instead, she focused on her childhood, which had been a very happy time for her.

"Well, I grew up in Michigan, just outside of Ann Arbor," she said. "My parents were both professors at the University of Michigan. Life is so different in the north. We spent our summers at the beach like here, but the winters were full of fun things to do like skating and skiing. I couldn't decide on one activity, so I tried them all. And since I was an only child, my parents spoiled me. I had a very happy childhood indeed."

"Where are your parents now? Do they still live in Michigan?"

She flinched at his innocent questions. Of course, he couldn't have known the raw emotions they brought up in her. But she wanted to be open and honest with him, like he had been with her.

"No. They were killed in a car crash when I was twenty-one. They were coming home from a fundraising dinner, and their car slid on a patch of ice and collided with a transport truck. They died instantly." She didn't mean to tell the whole story. Somehow it just came pouring out of her, and Nick was such a great listener.

He slid across the seat to sit with her and took her hand gently in his. It was warm and comforting. "I'm so sorry, Lily. That is a tragedy no one should have to go through."

"It's okay," she said before being overcome with emotion. With all the changes in her life in recent weeks, she hadn't had a moment to think about her parents and how proud of her they would have been. Her mom and dad had always encouraged her to chase her dreams. They had died just after she had started dating Derek. She was glad in a way that they hadn't seen her crumble after her divorce, but they would have supported her as they always did. Lily's runaway emotions got away from her and tears slid down her cheeks.

"Shh," Nick said and wrapped his arms around her tightly, kissed her forehead, and then brushed away her tears with his fingers. She laid her head on his shoulder. The scent of his spicy aftershave calmed her as she inhaled a deep breath. It was good to be in his arms again, and she was glad she had told him one of her secrets. She just hoped her former life didn't push him away. Suddenly tired from her surprise rush of feelings, she closed her eyes for just a moment. Then she drifted off into a peaceful sleep with his strong arms encircling her.

Sometime later, a faraway sound awoke her. It was Nick, he was whispering to her. "Lily, wake up, we're almost there."

She sighed and opened one eyelid. For a moment, she was disoriented then remembered where she was and what had happened. Heat from her embarrassment warmed her cheeks. Nick had an effect on her that she hadn't experienced before. Lily was opening up to him in a way she never had with anyone else. As she looked up into his clear blue eyes she saw excitement and wonder, not the pity she had been expecting.

"Look," he said and pointed in the distance. "There she is, the Moonlight Queen. Isn't she magnificent?"

He was talking about the cruise ship. Lily looked out the passenger window and saw in the distance a brilliant white and black vessel docked in the harbor. It was enormous. Bigger than she imagined. It was taller than her apartment building and looked very impressive. It had more decks than she could count, and it gleamed with a fresh coat of paint.

The rain had stopped, and the sun was beginning to show itself. It was going to be a beautiful day.

"Yes, I see it," she said and laughed. "It looks very grand. I can't believe how big it is. It's much bigger than any of the other cruise ships I have seen. I can't wait to get on board and see the rest of the vessel. It will take me days to find my way around, maybe weeks."

"You will discover your way around in no time. And it is all one big loop, so if you get lost just keep walking back to where you started."

"I'll try to remember that when I get hopelessly lost," she said and smiled.

Just then, the car pulled into the parking space reserved for limousines near the crew entrance to the ship. The driver got out and unloaded their bags. The sky had fully cleared by now, and the sun was high in the sky. Lily was now wide-awake and very excited. She was about to board her home for the next year.

"Okay," Nick said. "Let's get going."

The driver opened her door and she stepped out into the bright sunshine. She squinted. Her sunglasses were packed away, but she couldn't remember where.

"Have a safe and wonderful journey to paradise," the driver said to the two of them.

They gathered up their bags and headed for the ship.

"Well, Lily, we need to split up now and go our separate ways. You have to go and get registered in the new employee's line right over there." He pointed to the left of where they were standing. "I'll catch up with you later."

"Sure," she said and tried to hide her trepidation about being left alone. *Stop it. He's not going to hold your hand for the entire year.* She was a grown woman and could handle this. Lily hadn't been able to take in the enormity of the ship and the size of the crew until they had pulled into the port. She took a deep breath and made her way over to her section.

"Lily…" Nick called as she was walking away. She turned toward him. "Not so fast," he said and closed the distance between them. He wrapped his arms around her waist, pulled her close, and then pressed his lips to hers in the middle of all the hustle and bustle around them. The crowd faded into the background and she swooned, taken by surprise. As she closed her eyes and kissed him back, it was like they were the only two people in the world. She reached up and ran her hands through his hair. He sighed and pressed her tighter to him.

She could feel his strong muscles beneath his clothes. His tongue explored her mouth when she opened for him. She tasted strong coffee with sugar. They stood, locked in a tight embrace for a few seconds longer and then their lips parted. He smiled that beautiful smile at her again.

"Now that you have something to remember me by I'll let you go, but only if you promise to have dinner with me tonight."

"Yes, of course," she blurted out. "I mean sure. That would be nice."

"Great, I'll text you the details." He released her and stepped back. "Now get going, you don't want to be late on your first day."

Then he was off, and Lily stood staring after him for a long moment. Her entire body tingled from his touch. Not only was a fierce attraction there, she had gotten to know more about him on the limo ride over.

She was being swept away with him into a dream world, but she needed to be careful. She had a lot of work to do to get her new career started. With a sigh, she headed over to the long line and prepared to wait patiently for her turn.

Chapter Three

Two hours later, an exhausted Lily was trudging down a long hallway on the second level of the ship looking for her room. After she'd filled out more paperwork, she was told she would be sharing a cabin with a girl from Jamaica who was the tour manager for offsite excursions. Her name was Alecia Jones, and she had worked for the cruise line for the last two years.

The Caribbean Paradise Corporation had a program in place to match new employees with experienced workers who would help them acclimate to their new environment. Lily hoped Alecia was nice and was looking forward to meeting her even though what she wanted was a nap. Glancing at her watch, she calculated she had about an hour to get settled and then they were scheduled for orientation.

She reached her cabin at the end of the long hall. Music echoed from the other side of the door. She inserted her key card into the slot and watched as the light turned from red to green and the lock disengaged. Then she opened the door into a small room with twin bunk beds taking up the far left wall. There was a desk and two wardrobes. To the right there was a small vanity with a sink and next to that a door, which she assumed was the bathroom. Lily couldn't remember if she had ever seen such a tiny living space!

She spotted a young woman with a beautiful

mocha complexion and long dark hair sitting on the bottom bunk. The girl jumped up and bounded over.

"You must be Lily. I'm Alecia, and I am so pleased to finally meet you. Here, let me help you with your bags." She took her luggage and set it on the floor by the bed.

"Thank you. I'm very happy to meet you too. I've been waiting to start my new life on the Moonlight Queen for a while now. I hear you are cruise-ship alumni. It must be a pretty exciting life."

"It is fun for sure. Don't worry about being new. I will show you around and help you get organized. Then we will talk about Captain Nick Becket. I saw you with him when I was waiting in line. You have to be careful of him girl, take my advice on that one."

"What do you mean? I met him at the interview, and he picked me up on his way here, but I don't know him very well." She didn't want to lie to Alecia, but they had just met and she didn't want her to get the wrong idea.

"Well, you may want to keep it that way. He was a real playboy when we worked together on the Sunlight King last year, and he is already making a name for himself on this ship. Anyway, enough about him. Let's get you unpacked."

"All right," Lily said as she tried to digest this bit of information about Nick. She would have some questions for him at dinner tonight.

The girls spent the next hour organizing their room and chatting about the ship and home life. Lily told Alecia about quitting her horrible job and running away to paradise. Alecia told her about growing up in Jamaica and helping her parents run tours on the island.

She had two brothers and working in the family business led to an opportunity to work on the cruise line.

By the time Lily finished unpacking, she was famished. The girls went for a quick lunch at the cafeteria. They both dined on delicious lasagna, salad, and garlic bread. Then they headed up to the auditorium for the orientation.

Prominent crew members were onstage and they each talked for a few minutes about the ship and their role. Then they welcomed everyone on board. Lily was mesmerized when Nick got up to speak.

"Welcome all Caribbean Paradise crew members, new and returning to the Moonlight Queen, our newest ship in the Royal Class family of ships. She is one thousand, two hundred, and ten feet in length with a guest capacity of over five thousand. With two thousand crew members, there will certainly be a lot of exciting times ahead for all of us. I am looking forward to commanding this vessel and wish you all the best of luck in your area of expertise."

Nick went on to describe the ships amenities and unique features. Lily found she could listen to the sound of his deep sexy voice forever. But once again, she reminded herself not to get too attached. After the session, they were free for the rest of the day and had to report to their individual job assignments the following morning.

Alecia wandered off to see some of her friends, promising Lily she would catch up with her later. Lily made her way to the front of the stage where Nick was standing around with a few officers in crisp white uniforms. He had changed into his uniform as well and was looking very regal. He noticed her and motioned her over.

"Lily," he said and put an arm around her. "This is my first officer Daniel Lee and my second officer Mark Forde." He gestured toward the two men. They were both young and good looking.

"Hello, it is very nice to meet you," Lily said and shook both their hands. "It was a great presentation everyone put on today. I am looking forward to working on the Moonlight Queen." Both men said hello and smiled at her. She was trying to be polite, but she couldn't keep her gaze off of Nick.

"Well," he said to his officers. "Please excuse us. I have promised Lily a tour of our magnificent ship." He took her hand and led her out of the auditorium.

****

They wandered arm in arm around every floor, peeking into the lavish suites and laughing like school kids.

"Wow, these rooms are gorgeous," Lily gushed. "You could fit three of the cabins I share with Alecia in here."

"Really?" Nick asked. The crew cabins were notoriously small, but he didn't spend much time in any of them. He wanted to get her a larger cabin, but he wasn't sure if she would appreciate his interference. "Do you want to switch to a bigger space?"

"Oh no. It's fine. Besides, my roommate is super nice, so I think I'm in a good spot."

"Okay," Nick said and made a mental note to check in with her about the subject later. "C'mon, there's so much more to see."

Nick couldn't remember a time when he'd had so

much fun giving a tour. Lily was like a fresh breath of ocean air for him. She saw everything in a new unique and fascinating way. He took her to see the pool and the spa, and she was delighted.

"Oh, I can't wait to swim in the pool and then lounge in the sun. When can we do that?"

She looked so pretty and youthful, and her enthusiasm was infectious. Nick laughed and smiled down at her. He envisioned her in a string bikini and was instantly aroused. *Rein it in, Becket.* He wanted to take it slow with her from now on, but his body had other ideas. He refocused and answered her question.

"Everything should be ready by tomorrow, so we can come back then."

"Great! Where are we going next?"

Nick took her to see the skating rink. It was cold in there, and he hugged her close. He could smell the coconut and hibiscus scent of her perfume with her this close to him. He inhaled and savored it.

They could see their breath misting in the air. It was a large patch of ice considering it was on a cruise ship. He sighed as she snuggled into him.

"Wow, I can't believe there is a skating rink on-board. It's wonderful."

"Do you skate?"

"Yes, I'm rusty, but I'd love to try it. I grew up skating in Michigan. It's popular there, but I haven't done much of it since I moved to Florida."

"And we will, Lily, I promise you. Now you have to come and see my pride and joy."

She laughed again. "Let's go."

It was a short walk to his favorite part of the ship, the bridge, where he sailed the Moonlight Queen and did most of his other work. It was an enormous space. There were computers everywhere and dials of all shapes and sizes. A huge floor-to-ceiling window framed the front area and the view of the port was breathtaking. There were quite a few people milling about, checking things off on clipboards. They nodded politely at Nick but didn't interrupt him. He was suddenly nervous. What if Lily didn't think his work was as important as he did? Well there was only one way to find out. He looked over at Lily.

"What do you think?" he asked.

"It's fantastic and magical. I love it," she said. "I don't know how you keep track of all these controls. I'm getting confused just thinking about it."

"It takes time and a lot of training, but I can manage it pretty well now."

"You are a man of many talents," she said and giggled.

"Yes, I am," he said. A smile quirked the corners of his mouth. "Now, I'll walk you back to your cabin. I've got a few things I need to take care of, before our dinner date." He had made reservations at Jean Paul's Bistro. It was one of the restaurants that was opening up for the employees to try out their menu.

"Sounds good. I need to finish unpacking and find something to wear tonight."

"You'd look beautiful in anything." *Or nothing at all.*

She smiled in response and they walked hand-in-hand down to her floor.

When they reached her front door, she looked up at him.

"This is my cabin."

"Can I see inside?" he asked. He had to feel her lips on his before he left, and they were a bit too conspicuous out here in the hallway.

"Um, sure," she said. "But I have to warn you, it's a mess."

He wouldn't be looking at the room, only her. "No worries," he said. He didn't trust himself to say more.

She slid her key in the slot, and the door unlocked. Once they stepped inside, the two of them took up most of the free space.

"See," she said and gestured around the room. "Pretty small, huh?"

"Yes," Nick said, not registering the surroundings at all. His eyes were fixated on Lily. He gently cupped her face in his hands and brought her lips up to meet his. She reached around his neck and ran her delicate fingers through his short hair. He groaned at the contact and their lips met sparking a primal urge in Nick. He deepened the kiss, exploring her mouth with his tongue before twining with hers. As he leaned into her, the swell of her breasts pressed against his chest ramped up his desire. He ached to peel off her clothes so that he could caress and kiss every inch of her naked body. Nick got so caught up in the moment, he lost all track of time. Lily broke off the contact first.

"Nick," she said and breathed into his ear. "I think we'd better stop. Alecia could walk in any second now."

"You're right," he said with a sheepish grin. Her roommate had been the furthest thing from his mind. "To be continued?"

"Yes, to be continued."

"I'll see you later then."

"Later," she confirmed and opened the door so he could leave. He hesitated, not wanting this perfect moment to end, but it had. When he stepped outside, he shook his head to clear his thoughts. Unfortunately, it had little effect. She would be in his arms again soon; he would make sure of that.

****

Lily closed the door behind her and sighed. She had lost conscious reasoning as soon as her lips met Nick's. Despite her excitement, she was weary. It had already been a long day for her, and she wanted a short nap. She took the top bunk as Alecia had admitted she didn't like heights.

She closed her eyes and sighed. The tour was amazing, and her guide was pretty incredible too. The Moonlight Queen was an exquisite vessel, and it was already more like home than her small studio apartment had ever been.

Nick. What was she going to do about him? She was having so much fun on the tour that she hadn't had the opportunity to ask him about the rumors.

And now, she wasn't too sure how to bring up the subject. Was he really the playboy jerk that Alecia made him out to be? If so, her fears were well-founded. Or the rumors Alecia spoke about could just be false gossip. She had experienced her share of that while working at the insurance company. Well, she would just have to find out the truth at dinner tonight.

Lily dressed in a short, green silk dress for dinner. Her mother had always told her green brought out the color in her pretty eyes. Oh, how she still missed her parents, more than ten years after their death.

She stepped into gold sandals with three-inch heels

and looked into the full-length mirror on the back of the door. Her pretty honey-colored hair fell in waves down her back, and she added a touch of makeup to accent her outfit. Even with the heels, she was still much shorter than Nick. No matter, she could gaze up into his clear blue eyes for hours. She was falling hard for the gorgeous captain, but she'd better figure out if the feeling was mutual before she was in too deep.

As she was gathering up her purse and the directions to the restaurant, Alecia came back from visiting her friends. She whistled when she saw Lily and then smiled at her.

"Wow," she exclaimed. "You look great. I'm guessing you're not having dinner with me in the cafeteria tonight? If you are, you're way overdressed."

"Oh, no. I have other plans," she said, not wanting to admit she was seeing Nick. It was pretty clear Alecia didn't approve of him.

"Where are you going and with who?"

Alecia was not letting her get off without an explanation. Although Lily was an adult and knew she could handle herself, she appreciated that her new friend was so concerned about her.

"Well, Nick asked me to dinner earlier today, and I didn't want to cancel on him."

"Lily," Alecia said in a tone that Lily recognized. It was the one her mother had always used on her when she was in her wayward teen years. "I don't want to tell you what to do, but you really need to be on guard with this guy. Even though we just met, I can tell you are a nice girl, and I don't want you to get hurt."

"Don't worry. It's just dinner, nothing more."

"Okay, have fun then, but be careful. I am going

out later to catch a movie with some of the girls I met on the last voyage. If you want to join us, meet me back here after your dinner."

"Sounds great. I'll let you know." Then she was off on her way upstairs to find the restaurant.

Lily walked through the promenade deck to get to the bistro. It was the same deck her boutique was located on. It was elegant and magnificent. The glass walls and ceiling in this area were stunning. There was a beautiful staircase carpeted in what looked like dark blue velvet that led to the restaurants and night clubs. She climbed it feeling like a princess in a fairy tale, everything was so breathtaking.

As she approached the entrance, she paused. She could see into the restaurant and spied dark wood paneling and comfortable leather seating. There were a few people milling around, but it wasn't crowded. She approached the podium to give her name and stopped short.

Nick was standing a few feet away, looking gorgeous in a dark navy suit. He was gazing with adoration at a stunning female. Then he whispered something into the ear of the pretty hostess. She laughed and threw her arms around him. She was a young raven-haired beauty with short hair and an even shorter skirt. Nick leaned down and kissed the girl.

Lily couldn't believe her eyes. This was exactly what Alecia was talking about. She cried out loud and gasped for breath. Tears welled in her eyes and ran down her cheeks. She turned to flee the restaurant.

Nick saw her as she turned, and their eyes locked for a split second. He called out to her, but she didn't hear what he had said and didn't care. All she wanted to do was to get as far away from him as possible. Fresh air was what she needed. Spotting an exit through her tears, she headed down one level at a quick pace and out onto the deck where the walking track was located. It was deserted at this hour, and Lily was grateful.

The air was still warm, but a cool breeze blew around her. She could taste the salty spray from the ocean as she leaned over the railing and let the tears stream down her cheeks. While she gulped in the fresh air she chided herself. *How could this happen to me, again?* Nick had broken her heart before she had even known she had given it to him.

****

Nick ran up and down the promenade looking for Lily. He had lost sight of her in the hallway, and she didn't stop when he called her name. What an idiot he must have looked like to her with Francesca draped all over him. They were just old friends as far as he was concerned. Nevertheless, he'd let it go too far, and now he was afraid he wouldn't get a chance to explain.

He wandered up and down the ship looking for her without success. He ended up at her cabin door knocking incessantly until one of her neighbors peeked out to find out what all the fuss was about. Where was she? She didn't know very many people, and he didn't like the idea of her wandering around the ship alone and upset. He was furious and blamed himself as he was the cause of all of this trouble. Would he ever learn to behave like the gentleman Lily deserved?

He had experienced such a connection with Lily and hoped it might turn into something more. That was, if she gave him an opportunity to apologize. But he needed to change his ways. A girl like Lily Kingston didn't come along every day, and he wanted to hang onto her. He pulled out a pen and a piece of paper from his pocket and wrote her a heartfelt letter.

Nick slipped the note under her door and headed back to his cabin. He had lost his appetite and was no longer in the mood to socialize. Best just to turn in for the night. He hoped tomorrow would be a better day and that he could repair the damage he had caused.

****

Lily returned to her room a few hours later, exhausted. It had been an emotional roller coaster day, and she had reached her limit. She just wanted to get some sleep and try to forget about Nicholas Becket. Alecia had already gone out to the movies, so Lily had the small space to herself. She was finished crying. Out on the deck upstairs, she had poured out her heart on the gentle ocean breeze. As she changed out of her dress and into pajamas, she was calmer.

Who was she kidding? She wasn't in the same league as the beautiful woman she had seen all over Nick. Lily had been a fool to think he was interested in her. And to be honest with herself, she still wasn't sure if she was over her ex-husband. The emotions and heartache of a five-year marriage that ended in a bitter divorce, don't just go away overnight.

Seeing Nick kissing another girl had brought back memories of her failed marriage. Given the fact that Derek had cheated on her with a much younger woman, this latest betrayal only added salt to the wound. Perhaps she needed more time on her own before she was ready for a relationship. It was clear to her now that Nick wasn't serious about her or anyone, except himself and his huge ego.

She knelt down to pick up her sandals and noticed a crisp white paper folded on the floor. Wondering if Alecia had dropped it on her way out the door, she picked it up. *"Dear Lily,"* it began in strong, bold script. Oh no. It was a letter from Nick. She paused, not knowing what to do for a moment. Should she read on? Forget it, and forget Nicholas Becket. She was going to bed.

Lily pulled back the covers on her tiny bed and turned off the light. She climbed up to her top bunk, laid down, and closed her eyes. Her mind had other ideas, like rehashing her day. Just this morning she had been in Orchard Park, so excited to start her new life, and she was. This job was going to be very exciting, and she had already made a new friend. Then she remembered Nick and the way he had held her close when she had told him about her parents. There was real tenderness in his eyes for her, not fake. He had acted like he cared about her. Maybe she should read the letter and see what he had to say.

After she climbed from her bunk, she turned on the light, and walked over to retrieve the paper. It lay crumpled up on the desk where she had dropped it on her way to bed. She had been trying to forget that it was even there. Slowly she smoothed out the paper and read—

Dear Lily, I am so sorry for my behavior this evening. The woman you saw me with is just an old friend, but you would not know that by the way I acted. Please give me a chance to explain myself. Meet me for breakfast tomorrow morning at the Sunrise Café at seven o'clock. Please come, and I will tell you everything. You are unlike any woman I have ever met, and my heart aches knowing I have hurt you. Nick

She read and reread the letter three times. Was this all a big misunderstanding? Did he care for her? Should she meet him and give him another chance? The questions were swimming around in her head so quickly she became dizzy. The clock flashed bright on the desk beside her. She had been up for more hours than she could count and desperately needed sleep. She would decide whether or not to meet him in the morning. She turned out the light and crawled back into bed. Lily was so exhausted, she was asleep before her head hit the pillow.

****

Returning to his cabin, Nick could not get the look of surprise and hurt on Lily's face out of his mind. He was falling hard for this girl. Since meeting her a few weeks ago, he hadn't given any thought to the several women he had been dating. And he shuddered to think that he might have ruined it all in one flirtatious moment.

After tossing and turning for several hours, Nick called his sister Grace to ask for her advice. He was desperate to talk to someone about what had happened with Lily. Grace always had something insightful to say whenever he came to her with a problem.

"Oh Nicky," she said. "What have you gotten yourself into now?"

"I know, I'm such a jerk. I was already doing some serious thinking about my future and settling down. Then I met Lily, and the timing couldn't have been more perfect. Now I've gone and screwed everything up. I'm not sure if she will give me a chance to explain." He raked his hand through his messy hair and sighed. "What should I do?"

"Well, how about you wait and see if she responds to your note," she answered. "No sense getting worked up about it. You screwed up. You're only human and a man at that." He smiled at her attempt to cheer him up. She laughed, and Nick relaxed for the first time since his disaster of a night began. Grace was always teasing him about how women were so much smarter than men.

"Lily sounds like an intelligent woman. I'm sure she doesn't want to lose you either. After all, you are a great guy. Now, get some sleep. You don't want to look like a zombie tomorrow in case you get a chance to apologize to her."

"You're right, big sister. Thanks for listening."

"Anytime, baby brother."

They talked for a few more minutes. Their conversation ended with her making him promise to bring Lily back to St. Petersburg to meet the whole Becket clan if they were able to patch things up.

****

Dawn was approaching, and Nick hadn't slept well. Since he wasn't going to get any more sleep, he rose from his large king-size bed, stretched, and looked around his spacious room. An award winning designer had decorated the living space in muted blues to match the various hues of the open ocean.

He threw on some shorts and a T-shirt to go for a run on the track. Needing to clear his head after his sleepless night, a quick jog would work wonders. It had always helped him to relax and burn off some nervous energy. Today he definitely had more than his fair share of that.

He headed out of his suite and down two floors to

the track. The only people he saw were the night cleaning-crew, and he was thankful for that. The ladies were polite and just nodded at him. He returned their gesture and headed on his way, not in the mood for conversation. Reaching the area that encircled the entire third floor perimeter, he found the place was deserted this early in the morning. That was just the way Nick liked it.

He put in his earbuds and lost himself in beat of the music. As he ran the track, his mind relaxed. The wind was light and he could smell the salt of the ocean in the air. He was now feeling better and more in control of his emotions. Ten laps later, he was calmer and headed back to his suite to get ready for his breakfast with Lily. That was, if she accepted his invitation.

Back at his cabin, he walked into the small kitchen and switched on the coffee pot. His suite was luxurious with tasteful furniture. It boasted a large fireplace and entertainment unit. It was the biggest suite on the ship, and the space was too large for just him.

During past voyages when he had a similar cabin, his place had been the party hotspot with an endless parade of girls and booze. He had left most of the ship's care to his first and second officers, but the recent events with his father in particular, had changed his perspective. He needed to be more serious about his life and his career.

And now he had met Lily. She was one special woman, and he could see having a future with her if things worked out. Would she meet him for breakfast? Well, he'd better get ready, just in case. He showered, shaved, and put on his uniform. The quick walk to the restaurant would calm his frayed nerves, and he wanted to get there before her to get a quiet table with a stunning view. Waiting for a table, he tried to figure out what to say to her and settled on just telling her the straight truth.

Ten minutes later, Nick sat fidgeting in a quiet corner of the Sunrise Café. The waiter came to ask if he was ready, but he wanted to wait and see if Lily would come before he ordered something to eat. They both had a busy day ahead of them, so this might be their one chance to talk. Although he wasn't a religious person, he murmured a small prayer asking for her to show up.

****

Lily had been up for hours debating whether or not to meet Nick for breakfast. Alecia was still sleeping, so she got dressed in a smart navy suit with a skirt that ended just above the knee. She tied her hair up in a neat bun, all while trying not to make too much noise. Then she headed out of her cabin at a quarter to seven. Just before dawn, she had made up her mind to hear what Nick had to say and go from there. She had to get up and report for work at eight o'clock anyway, and besides, she needed to eat. As Lily headed into the café she almost lost her balance when she saw him.

Nick was dressed in his stark white naval uniform. He looked fresh and was clean shaven. His short blond hair was spiked, his blue eyes were shining, and he was wearing that breathtaking smile. She recovered the majority of her self-control and put what she hoped was a neutral look on her face, but she was finding it difficult. He was so striking; it was hard not to smile in return.

Nick got up and rushed toward her the moment he

saw her. He took her hand in his, and she couldn't resist his tender touch. It was warm and comforting.

"Good morning, Lily, I'm so glad you could make it. Please come sit down. I already got us a table." He was rambling on, but she just let him talk. He took a deep breath as they approached the table.

She eyed him with an expression that she hoped was cool and confident. "Good morning, Nick," she said and took the seat across from him.

"You got my note," he carried on. "Thank you for coming. I can explain everything."

"Well, let's order breakfast first," she said. "I'm starving since I missed dinner last night, and I don't want to be late for my first day on the job."

"Of course," he said. "What would you like to eat?"

"I think I'll have some eggs and toast, and then I would like to hear your explanation of last night's events," she added. She couldn't keep her unchecked anger out of her voice as she flashed back to the scene with Nick and the girl last night.

He didn't respond to her right away. Instead, he signaled the waiter, and they ordered. He asked for an omelet and fried potatoes. Lily wanted coffee, and he got an orange juice. Then he took another breath as he gazed deep into her eyes.

"I've never met a woman like you, Lily. I meant every word I wrote in the note to you. You are smart and sexy, and I think we have a deep emotional connection. The girls that I have dated in the past are only interested in partying and having a good time. And to be honest, I was of the same mind, until recently. Then things started to change for me. When I met you, I started to see another side of life. One I want for myself. Yesterday, I was acting like my old self, flirting with the hostess. We are just friends, but of course you couldn't have known. And for a moment, I forgot the new vision for my life. It includes you and only you. I promise, if you give me another chance I won't disappoint you again."

Lily stared at him for a long moment. She was impressed with what he had to say, and he sounded very sincere. Should she give in to his wishes? After all, people do make mistakes, and he was only human. He wasn't like her ex-husband who hadn't apologized for anything during their entire relationship.

Her head and heart debated for another moment while Nick sat across from her, looking uneasy. She finally took pity on him and spoke.

"Nick," she said and paused. His brilliant blue eyes were riveted on her. "I really do like you, and I want us to get to know one another better. I suppose I may have overreacted, but I have reasons that I'm not ready to talk about right now. The point is, I'm not going to accept you or any man dating me and kissing other women. For some younger girls it may be acceptable, but I am past the stage of casual relationships. I only want to spend time with someone who wants one woman…me. So if you think that person is you, we can start over."

"Yes, Lily," he said as he let out a long exhale. "That is exactly what I want." Then he rose, crossed to her side of the table, and pulled her up into his arms. He leaned down and put his mouth on hers. It was a soft, gentle kiss, and she returned it with a passion. They stood this way for several minutes, then he hugged her close, and whispered in her ear. "Thank you."

They finished their breakfast and then it was time for them to get to work. Nick smiled at her. "Let's try dinner again tonight. Just casual, in my cabin, no distractions. Does eight o'clock work for you?"

She smiled back at him. "Yes. That sounds perfect."

Chapter Four

Lily was very busy in the boutique on her first day as manager. She met with her two employees, Nancy and Rosa, and the marketing supervisor Sandra, who was her boss. Her staff were young, very nice, twenty-something girls, and Lily couldn't help wondering if they were acquainted with the infamous Captain Becket. But she was too busy to think about it for long. Besides, Lily was going to keep a close eye on them for work purposes, of course.

They stocked the shelves and had a crash course on how to work the new computer system. The boutique was elegantly appointed with smooth oak floors and it was painted in a soft taupe. There was a section for souvenirs, T-shirts, key chains, and mugs with the ships logo emblazoned on them. In the back was a section of fine jewelry in glass cases as well as the duty-free counter.

The time flew by, and then her first day as a Caribbean Paradise employee was over. After her shift, Lily headed back to her cabin to get ready for dinner. No fancy dresses tonight. She wanted to be her relaxed, casual self. Lily also wanted to check in with Alecia since they hadn't seen each other all day. She was tired, but looked forward to seeing Nick. As she was changing into comfortable shorts and a tank top, Alecia came back to the cabin.

"Hi, Lily," she said. "How was your first day on the job?"

"It was great. Pretty hectic. There is lots to learn, but I enjoyed every minute. How about you?"

"It was good too. A bit hard to get back into it after such a wonderful vacation at home, but give me a couple more days and I will be back to normal. Do you want to have dinner together, or do you have plans with Nick again? By the way, how was last night? We didn't get a chance to talk, but you were home before me and already asleep when I got in."

"Oh yeah, sorry I missed you. Dinner was great," she lied. She hated to deceive anyone, let alone a new friend, but she didn't want to get into it since she had already resolved it in her mind. "Yes, I'm seeing him again tonight."

"I'm glad you are having a good time with him. Just be careful, girl. I hope he has changed his ways for your sake, but I'm not totally convinced of that yet."

"I'll keep that in mind, thanks. See you later." She waved good-bye to Alecia and was out the door and headed off to the eighth level of the ship and Nick's cabin.

****

Nick was pacing around his cabin and glancing at his watch every few seconds. He was edgy and nervous as he waited for Lily to arrive. He had experienced a busy day with lots of meetings and the last-minute details of studying maps and weather patterns, consulting his officers, and charting the course for Saturday's maiden voyage. Those were the parts of his job he enjoyed the most, but the pressure was on to make this trip the best in Caribbean Paradise history.

After he finished work on time, he went back to his cabin to get ready for his date. He had changed out of his uniform, showered, and shaved. Now, all that was left to do was wait. Dressed in casual dark khaki cargo shorts and a gray T-shirt, he tried to relax.

Nick wanted the evening to be light and fun, the exact opposite of what he had planned and failed to carry out last night. What a mess that had turned out to be. He was so relieved Lily was willing to give him another chance. He wasn't going to screw it up this time.

He walked over to the mini bar and poured himself a scotch. The smooth amber liquid burned on the way down his throat, and he sighed. Lily was one special woman. She was unique in many ways and in all his years of dating, a woman hadn't ever affected him quite this way. He cared for her, and the fact he was falling for Lily was sinking in. It scared and excited him at the same time. Everything had to be perfect tonight.

Nick had ordered a gourmet dinner from the seafood restaurant on the ship. The meal was a lobster and shrimp feast. He hoped she would like it as he had forgotten to ask her if she ate seafood. There was a soft knock at the door, and he leaped up with a start. He hadn't been this nervous since he was an awkward teenager and new on the dating scene.

He rushed to the door. When he'd taken a deep breath and regained his composure, he pulled it open, and there stood Lily. She looked lovely, dressed in casual clothes like him, but still gorgeous. Her long blonde hair was loose and wavy hanging down her back. Her bright green eyes were searching his, and she smiled. He gave her his winning Becket grin in return.

"Hi. Please, come on in." He ushered her inside.

"Wow," she said. "This place is gorgeous. Your front hall is bigger than my entire cabin." She looked around at the gleaming cherry wood floors and the enormous windows. There were sliding glass doors that looked out onto a huge terrace. There was a black leather sofa, love seat, and matching chair organized around a beautiful fireplace, which was also done in the dark wood. Nick took her hand and led her over to the sitting area.

"I know," he said. "Most of the crew cabins are pretty small. I'm lucky with such a large space." He stopped short of offering to get her the better cabin he had asked her about yesterday on the tour. He could have done it with ease, but he didn't want her to feel like he was making decisions for her. If he brought the subject up, it might create distance between them. He didn't want any tension to ruin tonight. It was a discussion for another time.

"Can I get you a drink?"

"Yes. I would love some wine if you have it."

"White or red?"

"White, please."

"Sure, coming right up." He walked over to the fridge and pulled out an expensive bottle of Riesling. After pouring them both a goblet, he brought the glasses over to the antique wood table beside the couch. She accepted the glass and sipped the wine.

"This wine is bright and crisp. Very nice."

He was impressed she recognized a good vintage wine.

"Yes, it's one of my favorites."

"How was your day?" he asked her. Once again he

was amazed he cared about what she had done today and how she was feeling. Of course, he had often asked his other lovers about their respective time apart from him, but while they were answering, he wasn't listening. He was usually devising ways to get them into bed, and the sooner, the better. Lily, once again, was different.

"It was good. Busy, but good. The shop is going to be a great place to work. I spent most of the day ordering supplies and setting up the stock. Then I did some work with the computerized cash system to get it set up. How about you?"

"Well," he said. "I spent most of the day in meetings to set up the launch and course." *And thinking about you.* "Let's go out to the terrace, dinner is all set up." He took her hand and led her through the glass doors. Earlier that day, he had the wait staff from one of the restaurants set up a table for a romantic candlelight dinner.

"This is amazing," she said as she followed him outside. The beautiful table was set for two with fresh flowers, stunning silverware, and expensive dishes. As far as balconies go this space was large, looking more like a small backyard than a terrace on a cruise ship. There was a hot tub, sheltered by a lattice fence in the corner and several lounge chairs with plush blue cushions were placed for a perfect view of the ocean.

"Oh, my goodness," Lily exclaimed. "This is more elegant than your living room."

Nick just smiled and watched her as she took everything in. The sun was just beginning to set and the water was gleaming. It was a splendid evening, and he was having a fabulous time getting to know more about her.

Their dinner was wonderful. Lily gushed about how much she loved the lobster and shrimp accompanied by steamed vegetables and rice. As they were finishing up, she looked at Nick with an expression that he couldn't quite read. Before he could question her, she spoke.

"Nick," she said. "Thank you very much for this enchanting evening. I can't remember the last time I was so happy and content. Well, I guess I'd have to say the last time we had dinner." She laughed, but her voice then became serious. "I hate to ruin the mood, but I feel like I need to tell you something."

He looked at her with tenderness in his eyes. "Lily, you can tell me anything you want to. It's not going to change the way I feel about you." But her somber tone worried him. He had no idea what she was about to reveal.

"Okay," she said. "Well, I used to be married. I was happily married for five years. My former husband was a law student, and I helped to put him through school. Then we moved to Florida so he could set up his law practice, and I supported him again. Just as we were getting on our feet, financially and otherwise, Derek suddenly left me for another woman. He divorced me to run off with his much younger personal assistant. I was devastated to say the least." There were tears glistening in her eyes now, and one slid down her cheek. Nick reached over and brushed it away with his thumb.

She continued, "So yesterday, when I saw you kiss the hostess it brought up some terrible memories of the last few years of my life. I know I may have over reacted, but I guess it still hurts after all this time. I just wanted to tell you that."

"Oh, Lily," Nick said. "I can't tell you how sorry I am. What a jerk I was. Now it all makes sense to me. I feel like I have betrayed your trust. What can I do to make it up to you?"

Nick was caught off guard by her surprise confession. But given his somewhat colorful past, he was not in the habit of judging people, and Lily was no exception. What mattered was that she was here now.

"You're doing it right now by being so honest with me. Let's keep the lines of communication open so we can spend our time enjoying each other instead of arguing, okay?"

"That sounds perfect," he said. Then he changed the subject as he always did when the conversation got too intimate. "Now, let's enjoy that fabulous key lime pie the chef brought."

After they ate, they got up and walked around the large balcony taking in the view of the port. He had put on some soft romantic music, and the low tones flowed from the speakers. The sun had set, and the night was clear and bright. Soft lights twinkled in the distance, while a cool breeze brushed their skin.

He took her in his arms, and they slow danced around the deck. "Lily Kingston, you are one beautiful woman," he said to her.

"Why, thank you, Captain Becket."

They laughed, drinking each other in, and he wished time could stand still. That they could be stuck in this perfect moment forever.

He searched her gaze for any sign of apprehension but saw none. Her emerald eyes glittered as she smiled up at him. With a gentle touch, he took her face in his hands and leaned down to kiss her. Like the night at the hotel, her lips were soft and warm. Memories of their passion filled lovemaking came flooding back, and desire rushed through him. They shared a long and luxurious kiss as they danced around the balcony, holding each other in a warm embrace.

When they finally came up for air, he sensed that she was hesitating. *Time to slow it down, Becket. Take it easy.*

"Would you like to go for a dip in the hot tub?" he asked. He was trying in vain to keep his voice level, but the kiss had heightened his need for her.

"Um…" she said. "I would love to, but I didn't bring my swimsuit."

"I got you one," he answered and tried to sound casual, but failed.

"What?" she said with surprise in her voice.

An uncomfortable dread rose in him, and he tried to stamp down the panic. He went on, trying not to babble. "I had to pick up a few things for the voyage, and I came across a bikini. It matched your eyes, so I bought it for you. It's hanging in the bathroom, if you want to go have a look at it and try it on." It was her size and would look divine on her, but he didn't mention the obvious. She looked too uncertain, and he didn't want to alarm her further.

"Well, okay," she finally said. "Meet you back out here in a few minutes?"

"Sure, the bathroom is just down the hall, go past the master suite and turn right. I'll turn on the spa and check the temperature."

She smiled in response and headed inside. Nick

blew out a sigh of relief and raked a hand through his hair. Their kiss had held so much passion, he wanted to throw her down on the nearest lounger, tear off both their clothes, and have his way with her. He had to go slower with her. She wasn't one of his one-night stands whose names he barely knew, before they ended up naked beneath him.

He would try to hold back his longing for her, but it was going to take everything he had, and more. Although he ached to have her in his bed, he firmly reminded himself for the hundredth time, he wasn't going to push her tonight. She was finally back in his arms, and he was going to make sure she stayed there.

****

Lily wandered back into the spacious suite and looked around. This place looked like something from those fantasy house shows she loved to watch on television. There was expensive artwork depicting beautiful beaches on the walls and a few sculptures on the mantel, which probably cost more than her yearly salary.

However, she found it comforting that none of this opulence affected Nick. Sure he liked nice things, but he didn't flaunt it or try to impress her with them like her ex-husband always had. Derek was forever going on about how much things cost and insisted on driving an expensive sports car when they really couldn't afford it. She reminded herself to stop comparing the two men. Although it made her feel better to know that so far, they had pretty much opposite personalities.

She wanted desperately to fully trust Nick, but she just didn't want to get hurt again. Now she understood that she had overreacted after seeing him with the other woman last night due to her past. When she looked into Nick's stunning blue eyes, she saw someone who cared, someone she could trust. But still.

She shook her head to clear her thoughts and made her way down the hall. By accident, she took a wrong turn and found herself in the master suite. There was a huge king-size bed in the middle of the room. It was covered with ice blue silk sheets and a matching comforter. The plump pillows at the head of the bed looked so inviting, Lily almost reached out and touched them. There was a dresser and desk done in a rich black wood, and Lily was surprised to find the room neat.

Do I want to spend the night here, with Nick? Her stomach plummeted with what was either trepidation or lust. The attraction was there, she could feel it deep inside and hoped the feeling was mutual. She deserved to be happy, it was just that everything about this was so new. She pulled herself out of her wayward thoughts. Okay, enough snooping. She'd better get going or Nick would come looking for her and she wasn't ready to face him in his bedroom, at least not yet.

She crossed the hall to the bathroom, yet another richly appointed space. There were marble countertops done in off white with matching cabinets. The shower was a massive wall of glass that had a large rain-head faucet that Lily imagined would feel amazing on her skin. She saw the bikini hanging on the towel rack.

The suit was white with a cute emerald leaf pattern, and the bottom was a classic bikini, which she loved. She had to admit she would have chosen the same one, but the expensive label told her she couldn't have afforded to buy it. Oh well, it was so thoughtful of

Nick, she couldn't turn down his gift.

She stripped off her clothes and put it on. Looking in the floor to ceiling mirror, she discovered it looked good on her. How did he know her size? Well, he did have his hands all over every inch of her body the last time they were together. The memory made her shudder with pleasure. She pinned up her hair so it wouldn't get wet and grabbed a couple of fluffy white towels from the stack in the corner. Feeling prepared, for what she wasn't sure, she headed back outside.

Nick sat on the side of the spa waiting for her. He was bare chested and wearing black board shorts. Lily's heart fluttered at the gorgeous sight of his tanned sculpted torso and abs. She was trying to act casual, but he caught her looking at him and smiled.

"It looks great on you," he said as he gestured to her bikini.

"Yes, thank you, I love it. But, Nick, really, you shouldn't have spent so much money on me. I will try to repay you."

"No, you won't. Just enjoy it and this beautiful night. Come here." He held out his arms.

She walked into his embrace, and the contact of his bare chest on hers had a dizzying effect. He smelled of spicy aftershave, and his body was warm and inviting. He enveloped her, his light touch caressing her back. She swayed, overcome with sensation. He leaned back, a concerned look on his face.

"Hey," he said and looked her in the eye. "You okay?"

"Yes," she said as her face flushed with heat. Luckily, he didn't comment on her strange behavior.

"Let's get in," he said and took her hand in his.

She was relieved at his suggestion as the cool night air was beginning to chill her. They walked up the couple of steps, and he helped her settle into the water. The spa was the perfect temperature and looked like it could seat six people. A soft blue light gave the water the appearance of the ocean. The built in seats were comfortable, and the water was frothing as gentle jets massaged her back and feet. Nick climbed in beside her. She rested her head on his shoulder and closed her eyes. This was nice and relaxing. She could get used to this. Soft music was playing from the speakers near her head.

They spent the next few minutes in silence, unwinding and letting the warm water work its way around them. Lily opened one eye and peered at Nick. His eyes were closed, and his head was resting on the side of the tub. With his face so calm and relaxed, he looked younger. His short blond hair was wet and spiked, making him look like a surfer that had just come in from riding the waves.

It was at that very moment, she made a decision. She couldn't live the rest of her life hiding in fear. Fear of relationships, fear of love, but most of all fear of betrayal. She had stumbled; she had fallen, and had been terribly hurt in the process. Now she was back on her feet and wiser for the experience.

As she sat there gazing up at Nick, this gorgeous man whose arms she had fallen into just over a month ago, she felt herself break free from what held her back. Her past was from this moment on, in the past for good. She was ready to move on with her life. Her life with Nick.

She lifted her head up and placed a light kiss on his

cheek. He opened his eyes and smiled at her. He was being the perfect gentleman tonight, attentive to her emotions and respecting her boundaries. It was her move now.

She leaned in and pressed her lips to his. Wrapping her arms around his neck, she fisted her hands in his hair, and he deepened the kiss. He explored her lips with his tongue. The contact was gentle at first and then more persistent. She opened up to him and tasted wine and key lime pie.

Lily moved over in the tub so she straddled him. Her breasts pressed against his chest as she wrapped her long legs around his waist. They kissed again, deep and intense this time, and she could feel his arousal growing, pressing into her.

He broke off the kiss and tried to pull away from her, but she kept her legs in place, grounding them both.

"Oh, Lily," he said as he breathed against her ear. "What you do to me...what I want to do to you..." Then he looked down, his gaze locking with hers. "I think we should stop right here, before we do something we might regret in the morning."

"No, Nick," she said to him in a clear voice, so there would be no misunderstanding. "I'm not going to have any more regrets..."

"Lily," he said as he moved beneath her. He was trying to put some space in between them, but she held on tight. "Please, I want you to be one hundred percent sure this time. No more doubts. No sneaking out of my room in the middle of the night leaving me alone with a good-bye note. Despite what my body is saying right now, I'm willing to wait as long as it takes for you to be sure this is what you want. Now, let's get dressed, and I'll walk you back to your cabin."

He moved to lift her off him, but she resisted again.

"Nick," she said. "I want you, here and now. One hundred percent, and I promise I'm not going to change my mind about this."

"Are you sure?" he asked.

"Yes, Captain, I'm sure," she said and peeled off her bikini top to reveal her breasts to him.

He inhaled sharply, the exact effect she wished for. Then he took one of them in his mouth and placed a gentle hand on the other one. She moaned with pleasure as he kissed and massaged her flesh. His expert hands and lips were driving her mad with desire. He groaned and lifted her up.

"Let's go inside," he whispered. He stood up and grabbed a towel from the side of the spa. She rose and he wrapped her up in the soft terry cloth. Nick led her inside and shut the door behind them. They moved down the hall to the master suite, but he paused with his hand on the knob. He gave her a questioning look.

She took his free hand in hers and placed it on top of her hammering heart.

Lily looked at him, and his eyes were full of passion for her. "Yes," she said.

He opened the door. The room looked the same as it had before, all dark and masculine. He took her over to the edge of the bed where she wriggled out of her bikini bottoms and stood before him naked. She wanted him now, more than she had ever wanted any man. She broke away and sat down on the bed.

He pulled a condom out of the bedside table drawer and ripped it open. She took it from him and with a careful hand rolled it onto his manhood. A slow growl escaped his lips. She smiled as she had him right where she wanted him, and she wasn't going to stop now.

Lily slid onto the bed, pulling Nick with her. His resistance was non-existent now. He climbed on top of her and slid his smooth hands down the length of her torso. She closed her eyes as she reveled in the soft touch of his hands skimming her breasts, her belly, and then lower. As he parted her legs, he leaned down to kiss her. The touch of his lips to her bare skin was so delicate, but it was driving her mad with desire.

She was ready for him. She moaned his name as she writhed beneath him, clinging to the edge. He entered her, and she lifted her hips to meet him. They moved together in a steady rhythm, slow at first and then with more intensity. She came, crying out his name. He followed her a few seconds later groaning with the ecstasy that had overtaken them. In one swift motion, he rolled them both over. She was now on top with him still buried deep inside her. When she leaned over him, his arms encircled her, pulling their sweat-drenched bodies together chest to chest. Then he propped himself up on his elbows and gazed into her eyes.

"Lily Kingston," he said to her when his breathing returned to normal. "You're one sexy woman."

She smiled. "You're not so bad yourself, Captain Becket." She had done it. She had moved on and with no regrets.

Once they had rested for a few moments in each other's arms, he led her into the elegant bathroom. They made love again, this time under the rainfall shower. She was feeling very sleepy now, but content and happy. She sensed Nick was feeling the same emotions as her. Lily put on one of his T-shirts and climbed back into the big bed with him. Bare chested, he embraced her with his strong arms, and she cuddled into him, feeling warm and cherished.

When she looked up, he was staring at her. Then he spoke in such a low whisper, she almost didn't hear him.

"Will you still be here, when I wake up in the morning?"

He still doubted her. It made her feel sad, but she remembered that she had been the one to run out on him with little explanation the last time they were together. Now, it was her turn to prove she meant what she said.

"I will, I promise," she whispered back. "Now go to sleep."

He gave her forehead one more kiss and settled back against the pillow. As she lay with her head on his strong torso, she fell asleep to the steady beat of his heart and slept like a baby.

Chapter Five

Lily awoke the next morning to sun streaming in through the sheer blue curtains on the bedroom window. The bedside clock said it was almost nine. They had the morning to spend together, since neither had to go to work until later in the afternoon. She looked over at Nick who was still asleep with his arms around her. Lily liked the feeling of waking up beside him in his bed. It was so warm and soothing. She could see herself getting used to this.

She moved over a bit and untangled herself from his grasp, so she could get a good look at him. He was so young and handsome in his sleep. There was an innocent quality to his face that he tried to hide in his waking hours. He couldn't exactly command a ship with this look of boyish charm, but she loved seeing his unguarded side.

Lily couldn't resist reaching out and stroking his bare chest. It was so strong, as if he could protect her from the world and all its problems. That wasn't true of course, she was perfectly capable of taking care of herself, but the idea was comforting nevertheless.

He stirred and reached out his arms for her. Before she could suck in a breath, his hard muscular body enveloped her. Without opening his eyes, his mouth found hers, and they kissed passionately and deeply.

"Mm," he said when their lips parted. "I love

waking up to you in my bed. I think we should make a habit of this."

"Yes," she said, breathless from his kiss. "I think I could get used to sleeping beside you."

"Good," he said. "Me too."

He kissed her again and then opened his eyes. "You look so beautiful in the morning," he said and gazed at her with tenderness.

"Oh, I'm sure I'm a mess," she said and smiled.

"No way, you're gorgeous." He ran a smooth hand through her hair. "Are you hungry? What do you want for breakfast?"

"Are you cooking?" she asked. Nicholas Becket in the kitchen? This she just had to see.

"I can make a half-decent breakfast, as long as you want coffee and toast. Or we can get dressed and go to the restaurant if you want to." His words said they could go out, but his body language told her he wanted to keep her right where she was, for as long as he could.

"Let's have breakfast later," she said in a whisper. "I'm hungry for something, no, someone else."

He didn't need any more prompting as he moved to undress her. She lay before him, naked and full of need. He made quick work of his pajama pants. There was nothing separating them; they were skin to delicate skin. He kissed her with a tidal wave of passion, and her desire rose.

"Oh, Nick," she breathed. "I want you, with all my heart and soul."

"I want you too, Lily," he whispered and sighed a sound of pure pleasure. He climbed on top of her.

He ripped open a condom and rolled it onto his manhood. She stroked his hard erection and pulled a groan of raw need from him. He entered her warm, wet center, and she took all he had to give as she reveled in the intense connection they shared. Their own rhythm that was becoming familiar to both of them took over.

When they reached a fever pitch, she came, calling out his name. Hearing her seemed to be his undoing as he climaxed and shouted out to her in ecstasy. Then the only sound in the room was the sound of their breathing. First in pants, then a slow normal pace as they lay naked and wrapped in each other's arms.

Lily finally rolled over and looked at the clock. It was after eleven. They were both due at work by noon. She looked over at Nick. He looked content as he dozed beside her.

"Nick," she whispered. "We have to get up, or we will be late for work."

"Huh?" Nick said. He opened one eye and groaned at her. "Let's just skip work today and stay in bed, okay?"

"Um, no," Lily said with a little more force this time. "You are the captain of the ship, and I am a new employee, so we can't just not show up, let's get moving." She sat up and tried to move off the bed.

He grabbed her and pulled her back down into his warm embrace. She almost caved to this beautiful man. His arms were so warm and inviting, but it would look bad if she didn't show up for her second day of work. Nick could skip as many shifts as he wanted. He was in charge and owned the entire company. Unfortunately, she didn't have that luxury. She extricated herself from him with a sigh of regret.

"C'mon, time to shower."

"Okay," he said in a tone that said he was not

convinced her idea was a good one.

She took his hand and led him into the enormous bathroom adjoining the master suite. He looked like he was starting to wake up, but he had his hands and lips all over her, as if he wasn't thinking about work. To be honest, neither was she. Still, this was progress. At least they were upright and out of bed. She turned on the rainfall showerhead and let the warm spray work its magic to wake them both up.

He washed her hair with his delicate touch and once again, she almost gave up all rational thought and surrendered to him, but she reminded herself to stay strong. She needed this job and wanted to make a good impression on her new employees and her boss. Managing to get them both cleaned up without any further complications was almost a miracle, but she accomplished it.

After they were both clean and dry, she headed to the kitchen to switch on the coffee pot while Nick shaved and got dressed. Lily poured them both a cup and sat down at the small table in the kitchen. She inhaled and sipped the fragrant brew. It helped to wake her up from her dream-like world.

Nick emerged a few minutes later, looking very much like the commanding officer of the ship. He had a fresh white uniform on and he finally looked awake, but his bright blue eyes were still brimming with desire for her. He accepted the coffee she held out to him and took a big gulp. The entire time he drank, his eyes were fixated on her.

"It's not too late," he said to her with a mischievous look in his eye. "You know, to stay here all day and just enjoy each other's company..." He let the words hang in the air and Lily's previous courage began to crumble.

"Nick…" She stood and went over to him, looking him straight in the eye. "I would love nothing more, but you know how important this new job is to me. I can't afford to mess everything up."

"I know," he said. "You better go, while you still can."

"Thank you." She was relieved he understood. "Rain check on the passionate day in bed?"

"Yes. The next chance I get, Lily Kingston, you will be mine."

"Sounds perfect," she said and gathered her purse. "I have to run back to my cabin and change. I'll see you later," she said and headed toward his front door.

"Yes, you will," he replied and leaned down to kiss her. Their lips locked in a passion-filled embrace and their tongues found each other. She tasted coffee and toothpaste.

"Good-bye for now, Captain." She opened his door and exited into the hallway.

"Good-bye," he rasped in his deep sexy voice and then he gave her one of his handsome smiles that could melt an iceberg. She herself almost melted on the spot, but before she could, she hurried down the hall and away from the splendid captain of the Moonlight Queen, her new lover.

****

The next few days went by in a blur. Lily was busy learning everything she could about her new job and getting to know her new employees and cabin mate. Alecia was becoming a very supportive friend with similar interests and tastes. This was important, since they shared such a small space. Although they didn't spend much time in their cabin, since they were both so busy. Both girls liked things neat and tidy and tried not to get in each other's way.

Lily didn't get into too many details about Nick with Alecia. She wanted to keep him to herself, for now. Although, if Alecia had seen her and Nick around the ship together, she hadn't commented.

Lily had spoken to Victoria back in Orchard Park and told her all about Nick and the ship. Victoria couldn't have been happier for her. When Lily had described all the elegance and richness of the cruise ship, Victoria had been in awe. Lily promised to visit her, Tom, and the twins during her first week off. She was also working hard at her job, and her boss was very impressed with how she was handling the shop. She ran it like the professional she was and had her confidence back, for good this time.

In addition to working hard, she was spending as much time as she could with Nick. One night he took her to the Asian fusion restaurant on the ship. She had dressed up for this occasion in a little black dress and high-heeled pumps. Nick looked sharp in a gray suit with a matching tie and a white shirt. They made a beautiful couple. Nick was waiting for Lily outside the restaurant when she arrived.

"Wow," he said when saw her. "You look gorgeous."

"And you look very handsome, Captain," she said and took his arm in hers. "All the girls are talking about this place. I can't wait to try it."

"Let's go inside."

He led her into the dark restaurant and up to the

hostess stand. The young dark-haired girl, standing there in a short red dress, looked up in surprise when she saw Nick. "Good evening, Captain Becket, so nice to see you, again."

The woman completely ignored Lily, and Nick suddenly looked uncomfortable.

"Ah, good evening," he said. "We have a reservation for two."

The hostess then looked over at Lily as if noticing her for the first time. Nick was holding Lily tightly around the waist. Then her demeanor became ice cold, and she grabbed some menus from the stack beside her. "Of course. This way please."

She led them to a large table that seated about eight people. It was centered on a cooking stove where a chef was busy chopping vegetables. Lily noticed the woman had slipped Nick a piece of paper with his menu. Then, she stomped away.

"Do you know the hostess?" Lily inquired and eyed the paper.

"Err, maybe," he replied. "I'm not sure."

"Maybe?" Lily asked. She wasn't buying his story for a second. "What's going on Nick?"

She sat back and patiently waited for his reply. It was a little bit fun to watch him squirm because she was pretty sure the woman was an old flame of his. She was also sure he only had eyes for her now, she just wanted to hear him say it.

"Yeah," he said. "Her name is, um," he paused and fumbled for the paper. "Robin. We met on the last voyage, I think. Listen, Lily, it was nothing, so don't be jealous, okay? Wait, I'm going to give her back her number and tell her you are my girlfriend now."

And without waiting for her reply, he hopped out of his seat and made his way to the entrance. She saw him hand back the paper and gesture at Lily. The girl looked down, embarrassed. Lily didn't want the girl to feel bad, but she was tired of women falling all over Nick. She liked the way he had handled himself this time. He bounded back to the table and kissed her cheek.

"Lily, look, I'm really sorry about all of this and want to make it up to you. I don't really know this girl very well. You are the one I want to be with. Would you rather go and eat somewhere else or order room service? Please don't be angry with me." He stared at her with a look of concern etched on his gorgeous face as he waited for her to say something.

"Nick, I'm not mad. I'm very impressed with the way you handled this." She reached over and grabbed his hand. As he lifted her hand to his lips, he kissed each of her knuckles and need rose in her at his gentle touch. Relief was evident on his face at her response and she continued. "I want to stay and have dinner. If we went and hid in your cabin every time we saw an old girlfriend of yours, we'd never go out. Besides, this restaurant is supposed to be so much fun."

He frowned at her statement, but he couldn't argue with her about that point. Then he just smiled his megawatt smile and said, "Well let's order, I'm starved."

Lily was glad they stayed. They did not see or hear from the hostess for the rest of the night, and the dinner was wonderful. The waiters brought soup and Asian salad to start and then the chef cooked all of the food right in front of them. They ordered chicken, and he chopped it up, flipped it into the air, and they watched as it landed on their plate right next to some jasmine rice. He did many exotic tricks with his knives. It was thrilling. Lily and Nick clapped and cheered for the chef, as did everyone else at the table. Lily enjoyed herself that night and every night she spent on the ship with Nick.

Most of her nights were spent in his bed. They talked, laughed, and made love for hours and then slept. She was feeling tired a lot but chalked it up to her demanding job and her sensuous lover. She had experienced more things to smile about in this short period of time than she had in the entire last year living in Orchard Park.

****

The week flew by, and it was now Saturday, the day the ship was setting sail. Nick asked Lily to help him and the other crew members greet the passengers boarding the cruise line as the shop was closed until they were out at sea. She had agreed of course, as she was so easy to get along with. When she'd told him she was divorced, he had been shocked, although he tried his best not to show it. Whoever could have divorced her, was a fool indeed, but if it hadn't happened, he wouldn't have met her, so he considered it a blessing for him.

He was wearing his dress uniform with its black jacket and pants, looking very regal. Nick, his officers, and a dozen other crew members were all standing in the Great Hall. It was the entrance where the passengers first boarded the ship. They were met with elegance here, all the way from the polished mahogany wood floors to the enormous nautical themed stained-glass ceiling.

He straightened his hat and glanced around the space. He spotted Lily sauntering across the hall in her navy suit with hair tied in a bun. It was the standard uniform she wore while on duty. He smiled and waved her over. God she was beautiful. As he flashed back to the last few nights of passion that they had shared, his temperature and desire for her skyrocketed. She breezed over and smiled up at him.

"Good afternoon, Captain," she said. "Great day for the launch, wouldn't you say?"

"Yes, it is," he replied. Having her here might not have been such a great idea. He wanted to reach over and pull the pins out of her hair, so it would cascade down her back. Then he wanted to take her to the nearest secluded corner of the ship and have his way with her.

They had agreed to keep their relationship from the other employees for now, but he almost couldn't help himself. He leaned down and whispered in her ear. "Do you have to look so sexy right now? I'm trying to run a ship here, and all I can think about is what you've got hidden under your skirt."

"Oh, Captain," she teased. "I've just got my standard uniform on here, nothing to see."

"We shall explore that later, Ms. Kingston. Now let's get to work; we have guests to greet."

****

They separated then, he went to stand with his other officers, and she went to join her crew members. During the next few hours, Lily greeted passenger after passenger. After welcoming them, she directed them to the various check-in stations and let them know about the launch party on the Seaside deck at five o'clock.

She was planning to go as well, as she would be finished with her shift by then. Alecia said that they must go and check it out. Nick would be busy working until later tonight. She had promised to meet him for a drink at the casino when he got off duty.

Watching the cruise ship leave the harbor was exhilarating. As the ship left the dock, Lily imagined Nick on the bridge steering the ship out of the port.

"Isn't this amazing?" Alecia shouted over the cheering crowd and the noise of the sea.

"Yes, it's fantastic," Lily called. "Thanks for making me come with you."

"No problem, girlfriend. Besides, you can't spend all your time with the captain."

"I guess not," Lily reasoned, but she was feeling closer than ever to Nick and missed him when they weren't together.

"How's it going with him?"

Lily noticed Alecia still had a note of distrust in her voice. "It's going great," she said and then laughed. "I think he is changing his playboy ways."

"I hope so, for your sake."

"Me too," said Lily. She could taste the sea salt on the air as the ship picked up speed and the spray reached the deck. Nick had looked stunning in his dress uniform and a longing for him rose in her when she gazed at him. Despite the crowds of people coming and going during the afternoon, she often found Nick's gaze on her from across the vast hall. This small gesture made her realize how far she had come. She had turned a corner in her life with Nick, and she wasn't looking back.

After the launch, the girls headed back to their cabin. Lily had no idea what to wear to a casino, so she asked her roommate's advice. Alecia suggested she borrow one of her cocktail dresses. Since they were almost the same size, the pale blue chiffon dress with a halter neckline looked fabulous on her. She slipped on her silver heels and headed upstairs.

The Paradise Casino was a glittering array of lights and sounds. Since Lily hadn't been there before, she looked around in wonder. It was a large space decorated with various shades of orange carpet in a spherical pattern. Slot machines in various denominations flagged the entrance, and there were many others when she stepped inside. The game tables were located farther back, and the lounge was a spacious area with plush leather seating in tones to match the carpet. Lily was a few minutes early so she sat down at a table to wait for Nick.

She ordered a club soda. Nausea had been plaguing her for the last little while. It wasn't enough to keep her in bed, but she didn't feel like drinking alcohol tonight. She would wait for Nick to see if he wanted any food. She had eaten earlier and wasn't very hungry.

Lily took in the scene around her. There were various people of all ages scattered about the place. Everyone was dressed up in evening wear. Most of the men had tuxedos on, and the women wore elegant gowns. Everyone looked happy and excited. Then, she spotted Nick from across the crowded floor.

He looked divine in a black tuxedo with a white shirt and black tie. His short-cropped hair was spiked, and he looked so tall in that outfit. His easy smile and casual walk as he greeted passengers had Lily holding her breath in anticipation. She let out a sigh and took a few cleansing gulps of air. She had it bad for this handsome fellow.

He continued farther into the casino but was stopped every few steps by a passenger or a colleague, Lily wasn't sure. Everyone was dressed up, so it was hard to tell who was who, but she could see him looking up and scanning the crowd, hopefully, for her.

As if he could read her thoughts, their eyes met across the room. He smiled his breathtaking smile and attempted to make his way toward her. About five minutes and ten guests later, he was at her table.

"Good evening, Captain," she said, not sure if he wanted everyone in the place to know about them. She stood to greet him and was still quite a few inches shorter than him, despite her heels.

"Good evening," he said in his smooth sexy voice. Then he reached down and took her in his arms. He spun her around, and their lips met in a scandalous kiss. He kissed her deeply, right there in the middle of the casino. Lily was taken aback at first, but once Nick's lips were on hers, the background faded away, and all she could think about was the two of them entwined together as one.

When the kiss ended, the crowd cheered and clapped. Lily was mortified, but it didn't bother Nick in the least.

"Okay, okay," he said to the crowd. "Thank you. The show is over. Please get back to enjoying yourself at the casino and for the entire week aboard the Moonlight Queen."

The crowd echoed Nick's sentiment with a few hoots and hollers, then dispersed, going back to whatever they had been doing before.

He smiled at Lily and gestured to the chair beside her. "Hello, gorgeous," he said with a wicked grin. "Is this seat taken?"

"Well," she said. "I was saving it for my boyfriend, but you are a much better kisser than he is, so you can sit down. If he ever shows up, I'll tell him to get lost." She giggled.

"Why, thank you," he said and sat down beside her. "You look amazing, very beautiful. What a lucky boyfriend you have."

"I think so too."

He kissed her again, with much less fanfare this time, but no less intensity. She tasted fresh mouthwash and cinnamon gum. It almost took her breath away.

"Nick," she said, as she broke their contact with much regret. "Didn't you want to keep us under the staff radar? You're doing a terrible job, in case you didn't know."

"Lily," he said. He was almost as breathless as she was. "With you looking so beautiful in that knockout dress, I just had to let every man in here know, that you are mine, all mine. And the staff, well hell, I guess they will find out too."

"If you are sure…"

"I'm positive. Do I need to kiss you again to prove it?"

"Maybe later," she said and smiled. "I think this crowd has seen more than they can handle of us right now."

"Nonsense. But as you wish, my princess. Now, would you like to play some blackjack?"

"Well, I've no idea how to play, but I would love

to watch you in action."

"Splendid. Let's go."

He took her arm in his and led her over to the card tables. The blackjack table was busy, but there were a few vacant seats. A game was just wrapping up. Lily took a seat beside Nick and watched him in anticipation. She guessed he played cards the way he did everything else. He played to win.

The dealer nodded to him politely. "Good evening, Captain Becket. Would you like in on the next game?"

"Good evening, Sergio," he said to the dealer. "Yes, please. Changing one hundred." Nick pulled a crisp bill out of his pocket and handed it over. Lily stared in awe but didn't say anything to him. She couldn't imagine betting any sum of money, but Nick looked confident, so she sat back and watched.

The dealer changed the money and handed Nick five chips. He put them down and the dealer dealt him two cards. The first one was face up, a ten. She watched as Nick glanced at the other card with ease. The dealer's card that was upright was an eight. Lily couldn't see the dealer's second card. She had seen a bit of this game in movies and on television, so she tried to remember how it was played. She recalled that the closest person to reach twenty-one without going over wins the round. It was Nick's move. He looked so handsome, deep in concentration. She stayed quiet, trying not to distract him. The dealer had a serious look on his face as he waited for Nick to respond.

"Stand," Nick said and flipped over his other card. It was a nine. His total was nineteen. The dealer flipped over his card and it was a ten. The dealer's total was eighteen. He dealt himself another card. When he turned it over, it was a five. Sergio had gone over and gotten twenty-three. Nick had won this round. Lily clapped and cheered for him, and he planted a passionate kiss on her lips.

"You must be my good-luck charm," he murmured in her ear. "So stay right where you are."

"I'm not sure about that," she whispered back. "But you look so sexy concentrating on those cards, that I can't tear myself away."

"Not half as sexy as you do cheering for me. But if you keep it up, Ms. Kingston, I'll lose everything, because I can't stop thinking about what I'm going to do to you when we get back to my cabin."

"Oh, nonsense," she said. "Play a few more rounds since you are having so much fun. Then you can take me to your lair and have your way with me." A joyful smile played on her lips. She looked at him again and could tell he was debating what to do.

"Okay. But only if you keep cheering."

"As you wish, Captain."

Nick put all ten chips down on the table and the dealer dealt the cards again. This time Nick had a jack and the dealer had a queen face up. That meant they both had an even ten. She wasn't sure what Nick was going to do, but of course, she couldn't see the other cards so she just waited.

A small crowd gathered to watch from around the casino. Everyone wanted to know what the captain of the Moonlight Queen was up to. Lily watched him, and he handled it well, with the grace and politeness of a professional. She wasn't sure how she would feel about getting all this attention. She was pretty sure he was used to it by now, but it was a bit unsettling for her.

Nick made her feel more than comfortable, surrounded by people who wanted to talk to him, so she guessed it was just something she had to get used to.

She refocused her mind on the game at hand.

"Hit me," Nick said, as he requested another card. The dealer dealt them each another card so now they had three. This was getting interesting.

The dealer waited patiently for Nick to call out his play.

"Stand," Nick said.

Lily watched as all of the cards were turned over. He had a ten, a five, and a six, he had gotten twenty-one exactly. The dealer had a ten, a three, and a five so with eighteen Nick was the clear winner. Lily clapped and cheered again for him, making good on her promise.

He joined a third round, and she watched again in anticipation. She wasn't disappointed. He won again, this time getting a risky nineteen, but the dealer had gone over and gotten twenty-three. By this time, he had won, eight hundred dollars. He turned to Lily after his latest win. "Well, what do you think?"

"It looks like a lot of fun, especially when you are winning. Are you going to keep playing?"

"I think I've had enough for tonight. Besides, I have other plans for us that don't involve a captive audience. And I always say, it's best to quit while you're ahead."

Lily smiled in response. "Good philosophy, Captain. I'm ready to go as well."

They got up from the table, and Nick thanked the dealer with a generous tip. When they walked over to the cashier, Nick was handed his winnings. Several people stopped him to say hello on their way out. He was polite but brief and didn't look like he was paying much attention to anyone but her. He had romance on his mind, the way he was holding her tight and caressing her back. A shiver of desire rushed through her at his delicate touch. They made their escape and headed back to Nick's suite with a passion in their eyes that was soon fulfilled behind the closed doors of his cabin.

Chapter Six

The ship made several stops on its voyage around the Caribbean. They had a few days at sea before stopping in St. Martin. Then it was on to St. Thomas, and the cruise ended with a day in the Bahamas. When the ship was in port, the shop was closed so Lily often had some free time to explore the islands if she wasn't assigned to other duties.

One day, when they had docked the ship in St. Martin there was a knock at her cabin door. Alecia had been up and out hours earlier as she had to oversee the island tours. Lily was dressed in a white bikini and a matching cover up. She was thinking about relaxing and hanging out by the pool since Nick had said he had to work. To be honest, she had been feeling a bit seasick since the ship launched, something she had not expected. She was ready for a day of rest that she hoped would help to alleviate her symptoms.

Lily opened the door expecting to see one of Alecia's friends. Nick was standing there instead, looking handsome in cargo pants and a blue T-shirt that brought out the sparkle in his eyes.

****

"Hi beautiful," he said to her. "There's been a change of plans for today. I switched shifts with Daniel. Grab your stuff. I have a surprise for you." He leaned down for a quick kiss, and she wrapped her arms around his neck.

He inhaled the coconut scent of her lotion and deepened their kiss. If this went on too much longer, he would just shut the door, take her over to her tiny twin bed, and make love to her all morning.

"Let's go," he said and pulled away with regret.

"Where exactly are we going?"

"C'mon, it's a surprise. But we have to hurry."

She agreed without further argument and got her things together. Then he led her down to the exit of the ship. When they got off there was a tour van and driver waiting for them. It was a gorgeous day. The sky was clear blue, and the palm trees dotted around the port were swaying in the gentle breeze. He led her over to a vehicle he had reserved just for the two of them.

"Oh, Nick. This is too much."

"No, it's not. This is my favorite island on the voyage, and I want to explore it with you. Can't blame a guy for wanting to have the most beautiful woman on the Moonlight Queen all to myself, can you?"

She laughed and threw herself into his arms. "No, I guess I can't."

"Great. Let's get going."

He took her hand and helped her board the van. The island was divided into two sides; French and Dutch. The tour guide told them the history of the island and pointed out important landmarks as they went along.

He spoke of the folklore surrounding how St. Martin was formed. When both the Dutch and the French divided the island, each side elected a walker who they sent to opposite ends of the island. They started to walk at the same time and when they met in the middle, the two sides were formed. The history and scenery were all fascinating to Lily. Nick had been on this tour many times, so he was content to sit back and revel in her excitement.

They toured both sides of the stunning island and wandered through the shops in town. She picked up some souvenirs to send to Victoria and her kids. They feasted on local cuisine and the island specialty, guava berry rum, for lunch. It was delicious.

Afterward, the driver dropped them off at a quiet beach. They swam in the warm ocean and walked for miles in the soft sand. Then Nick spotted a cove partially hidden by tropical plants. He spread out a blanket inside the small inlet, and he and Lily lay down next to each other.

"Lily, you are so lovely," he said, looking at her stretched out and relaxed on the blanket. "How did a guy like me get so fortunate to have found you?"

"I think it was fate," she said and grinned. "Ever since I fell into your arms at the job fair."

"Well it was my lucky day, that's for sure."

He leaned over and covered his body with hers. Their lips met in a surge of desire. He ran a hand up her bare arm and felt a shudder run through her body. Passion and need for her filled him. Their kisses intensified, and he tried in vain to reel himself back. It was becoming impossible.

He wasn't sure if she would want to be this intimate, given they were, more or less, in public. Although there were just a few people scattered along the beach, it didn't have the privacy of his cabin.

As if in response to his unspoken query, she tugged at his shirt. He tore it off, revealing the tanned skin of his chest to her view. She caressed his bare torso with her light, feathery touch, which dragged a sigh from his lips.

"Maybe we should get going," he said. It was the opposite of what he wanted right now, but he wasn't sure about Lily. It pained him to say the words, but he was desperate to try and be the gentleman she expected.

"Nick," she said in a breathless whisper. "Take me. Right here and now."

He hesitated. "Lily, are you sure you want to do this?" He didn't want her to have any regrets now that they were back on track. It wasn't worth the risk.

"As sure as I'll ever be," she said, as she peeled off her cover-up and bikini to climb on top of him, naked.

The tropical setting surrounding them only made her more exquisite. He slid off his swim trunks and grabbed a condom from his knapsack. Taking her breasts in his hands, he massaged her nipples. She whispered his name in ecstasy as she eased him into her warm ready body in a slow and steady motion. He savored the feel of her enveloping him. The ocean waves had a soothing rhythm that they matched as they rocked in unison. Pure rapture overtook them, and together they slid off the edge of reason and into paradise.

Afterward, they lay dozing in each other's arms listening to the gentle sound of the surf.

"This was quite the surprise, Nick." He didn't know if she was referring to the tour or the sex. He hoped it was the latter.

"Yes, it's been an incredible day."

"I just wish we had more time to spend here."

They rested in silence for a few more minutes

before they had to get dressed and head back since the ship would be leaving port. He made a mental note to remember this place so they could come here every time the ship docked and have their own private escape.

****

The weeks flew by, and it was now early October. Lily had been sailing with Nick for a month and was overjoyed. They were closer than ever. She was also working hard at her job, and her boss was very impressed with how she was handling the shop and her new responsibilities. Lily had implemented the new computerized cash system with ease and supervised her employees in a polite and professional manner. She had her confidence back both in her work and personal life.

The one thing that was bothering her about this entire voyage was her pesky nausea symptoms. They came and went without warning. She had tried some remedies Alecia had recommended such as ginger tablets and a seasickness wristband. It was manageable but still bothered her. She made an appointment with the ship's doctor. This hadn't happened on previous cruises she had taken as a passenger, and she was a bit concerned. Although she didn't want to make a big deal about it, she also didn't want it to interfere with her job.

She had Tuesday morning off, and the doctor had agreed to see her, so she went up to the mainstream deck, which housed some of the offices and the medical clinic. It was decorated in plain pale yellow tones. Most passengers didn't see this area of the ship, unless of course they got sick, so it didn't have the elegance that was evident in the rest of the vessel.

The clinic itself had stark white walls, and the nurse at the desk was all business as she ushered Lily into an exam room. Not one of the most fun jobs on the ship she reasoned, trying to explain the woman's behavior, but it made her uneasy. As she sat there waiting for the doctor in her panties and a paper gown, she became a bundle of nerves. What if something was really wrong? *Stop it right now, Lily Kingston. You are just being paranoid.*

The doctor's entrance interrupted her thoughts.

"Hello, Lily," said the physician as she looked at a chart. "I'm Dr. Peters. How can I help you today?"

The doctor was a young woman of Indian descent. She had long black hair pulled into a ponytail and wore a crisp white lab coat. Her professional look and empathetic smile helped to put Lily at ease.

"Well," Lily said. "I've been having quite a bit of nausea on the ship, so I wanted to come and see you."

"Good idea. The nurse had your doctor in Orchard Park fax your medical records to us. Your overall health is good. The nausea started when?"

"I guess pretty much from when the ship sailed. But it comes and goes."

"Do you feel it when you are off the ship?"

"Yes, sometimes."

"How are your periods? Regular each month?"

"No, not really. My cycle has been off, and I didn't get it last month. But I'm used to that. It's happened a few times before, so I'm not too concerned."

"Any weight gain?"

"As a matter of fact, maybe a few pounds. The food onboard the ship is really good, and I've overindulged for sure."

Dr. Peters then took her vitals, her blood pressure, and temperature. She frowned at the numbers but didn't make any comments.

"Lily," the doctor said and paused. "Do you think you could be pregnant? Have you had unprotected sex in the last three months? I see from your chart that you are single and not on any prescribed form of birth control."

"Pregnant?" Lily asked. "No, I don't think so..." Nick had always used condoms, hadn't he? Well, except for the first time, it had caught them both off guard. But it was just one time. Lily noticed the doctor was staring at her waiting for a response.

"There was one time in early August. But just once. It's not possible to get pregnant from one time, is it?" Lily didn't think so. After all, Victoria had spent six months trying to get pregnant before she had conceived the twins.

"Yes, it is," the doctor said. "I think we should do a blood test for pregnancy as well as anemia and check some of your levels. If you are pregnant and there is a chance you may be, it will affect how I treat you for the nausea. You can come back tomorrow for the results."

"Okay," Lily said, not knowing what to think, her mind was reeling.

"Let's not jump to conclusions," Dr. Peters said in a soothing tone. She was no doubt reacting to Lily's expression of terror, which she could tell, without looking in the mirror, was on her face. "Once we have the results, we can discuss your options. Do you want me to call someone to take you back to your cabin after the test?"

"No, I'll be fine," she replied and tried to regain her composure. What the doctor had said was true, and it was best not to panic just yet. She assured herself she wouldn't and was sure the doctor was mistaken about the pregnancy.

"Very well. Nurse Suzanne will be in to draw your blood for the test, and then I want you to rest for the remainder of the day. If you need anything else, just call the clinic. I will be here until five o'clock this evening."

"Thank you," Lily said as Dr. Peters left the room. *Oh no. This can't be happening to me.* The anxiety was creeping in again, but before her thoughts could get away from her again, the nurse entered. She took Lily's blood without any comment and sent her on her way.

Lily was supposed to work in the afternoon but found she was too shaken up. She called Rosa, one of the other girls at the boutique to fill in for her. She was more than happy to help Lily out by putting in some extra hours.

Lily returned to her cabin and found it empty. Alecia had said she had a packed schedule today, so they weren't going to see each other. Lily was relieved. She didn't feel like talking to anyone right now. Nick was working a long afternoon shift, so they hadn't made plans. Thank goodness, she had some time to herself to think. What was she going to do if she was pregnant? Nick hadn't mentioned children or even marriage to her. After all, they had only been dating for a short time.

Certainly, a baby didn't fit into her current lifestyle. She found herself exhausted from the worry and the what if's. A short nap would clear her head and re-energize her tired body. Putting on some soft soothing music and laying down on her bunk, she fell asleep to the quiet melody.

Several hours later, she awoke to an incessant knocking at the door. "Great," she muttered to herself. Alecia had forgotten her key, again. She got up and went to answer it. Opening it, she saw Nick, looking handsome as ever in his uniform. But he had an anxious look on his face that she hadn't seen before.

"Lily." He sighed and enveloped her in his arms. "Thank God you're all right. I went to the store to see you on my break, but you weren't there. Rosa said she was filling in for you and that you had been to see the doctor and weren't feeling well. I got worried and came straight here. Why didn't you call me?"

Lily had forgotten what a big mouth Rosa had. Oh well, she supposed he would have found out somehow. She made a mental note to be as vague as possible if she needed any more shifts covered. Looking up at Nick, she tried to sound as casual as possible. "It's nothing, really. Just maybe a touch of the flu," she lied. "It's been going around the ship. Besides, I know how busy you are today, so I just took a nap and feel better all ready."

"I don't buy it," he said and frowned.

"What? Why?"

"Lily, you are still the most beautiful woman on the ship, but you're not a good liar."

"Nick, I..."

He cut her off. "You don't look well. I know you are feeling sick even if you won't admit it to me. I'm taking the rest of the day off. You are coming to my suite to rest and have something to eat. I'm going to look after you."

"Nick, no," she protested. She didn't want to spend any time with him today. Her thoughts were too jumbled, and she was afraid she might say something she would regret later. He was right about one thing though; she was a terrible liar.

"I'm not taking no for an answer, so pack an overnight bag and come with me. Now."

There was no point in arguing with him. She had seen that look in his eyes before. He was being overbearing and stubborn, but she didn't feel like a battle today, so she acquiesced.

"Okay," she conceded and gathered her things.

Twenty minutes later, she was comfortable and resting on the king size bed in Nick's suite. She had to admit his cabin was much more airy and spacious. The large windows in the room eased her nausea, but she was bone tired from the stress of the day. She was wearing a cotton lavender pajama short set, and she was looking anything but sexy.

When they had gotten to his suite, Nick had called the bridge and gotten Daniel, his first officer to cover his shift for him. He had changed into casual jeans that sat low on his slim hips. He was bare chested as he paced around the room and looked at Lily with a worried expression.

"Maybe, I should call the doctor and have her come down and see you. You are still awfully pale, and I know you haven't eaten all day."

"No!" She sat up in bed. She was making the situation worse by her reaction and tried to recover her composure. "I'm fine. Besides, I have to go back and see her tomorrow anyway." *Now why did I mention that?*

"What? You didn't tell me that before. Well, I'm going with you tomorrow so we can get to the bottom of this."

She wasn't going to let that happen, but she didn't want to overreact and arouse his suspicions again. She would deal with it later. "Nick, really I'm okay. Why don't you order me some soup and a tea? I think I can eat now." She was trying to distract him by giving him something to do. "And then let's rest, I do feel tired again."

"Sure," he said. His gaze was still intense, but he made no further comment. Half an hour later, he brought dinner to her on a silver tray. It was fragrant chicken soup and green tea. He had ordered a turkey sandwich for himself. They ate quietly, each lost in their own thoughts.

****

After dinner, Nick cleared the dishes and then sat on the edge of the bed watching Lily. Twilight had begun to shadow the room. He was worried beyond belief about her. This surprised him as it showed him how close they had grown. She looked so small and fragile in his big bed. He wanted to wrap his arms around her and make her all better. He hadn't felt this way about any other woman, ever. She turned toward him and sighed.

"Come to bed," she whispered.

"Okay." He took off his jeans and slid under the cool silk sheets with her. As he placed his strong arms around her, he planted a soft kiss on her forehead and frowned. She was cool to the touch. He wrapped his arms around her tighter, trying to warm her up. He listened to the sound of her breathing become slow and steady as she relaxed and fell asleep. Concern for her swirled through him, and he wasn't sure he would get much rest. He hoped that she would be all right, because he was unable to imagine a future without her in it. Nick just couldn't admit that to her, yet.

****

Morning sunlight was streaming through the room when the high-pitched shrill of the telephone awoke them. Nick swore and grabbed the phone. He wasn't due on the bridge till later.

"Becket," he growled into the phone. "What? When? All right, don't touch anything else. I'll be right there." He slammed down the phone and jumped out of bed.

Lily turned to face him and opened one eye. "Is something wrong?"

"Lily, I'm sorry the phone woke you. I wanted you to sleep in. I have to run up to the bridge. One of the computers is offline. Are you going to be all right? Stay in bed and rest. I'll come back to check on you as soon as I can."

He didn't wait for a response as he ran into the bathroom to throw on his uniform. Making it back to her in seconds, he leaned down and planted a light kiss on her cheek. Then he rushed to the bridge.

****

Lily looked at the clock on the bedside table, sighed, and flopped back down onto the pillow. She did feel better this morning, but then her stomach tightened as she remembered her appointment at the clinic in an hour. At least she didn't have to fight with Nick about him coming with her to the appointment. What a relief. He had been so preoccupied with the emergency on the bridge that he had forgotten all about it. Thank goodness for small favors.

Lily got up, showered, and dressed in her uniform for work. The nausea had set in again so she couldn't eat much, but she managed some dry toast and juice. There was a mid-morning meeting she needed to attend, and she planned to go straight to the boutique after her appointment. She just hoped the doctor had good news and some medicine for her.

She scrawled a quick note to Nick telling him she was fine, and she would call him later. He would be annoyed that she wasn't here when he got back, but that was just too bad. She needed to get this sorted out for herself and the sooner, the better.

Lily's nerves were frayed again as she sat in the small examination room for the second day in a row. The confidence she had gathered over breakfast had evaded her as soon as she approached the clinic. The same nurse had gotten her settled in the waiting room and had the same demeanor as the previous day. At least the doctor was nice.

A few minutes later, Dr. Peters walked in with Lily's file in hand. "Good morning, Lily. How are you feeling today?"

"About the same. Did you get my test results?"

"Yes, I did. Lily, you are pregnant. That is the cause of your symptoms. All of your other levels, including the anemia test came back normal."

Lily froze. She refused to believe what the doctor had just said. "Are you sure?"

"Yes, the tests are conclusive. You are about eight weeks along. From your reaction, I'm guessing that this is not good news."

"No it's not. I've just started my new career. I don't know what I am going to do." Lily started to cry, she couldn't help herself. The doctor handed her some tissues.

"Lily," Dr. Peters said. "What about the father? Do you have a relationship with him? It is often helpful to have a partner here when we discuss pre-natal treatment."

"No, we're not together anymore," she lied. Well, they wouldn't be when he found out about the baby. Nick a captain, was a given. Nick a father, no way.

"Is there anyone I can call for you?"

"No, I'll be all right," she said but was anything but that. Her world was crumbling down around her, and she had no idea how to fix it.

"Okay," Dr. Peters said. "You need to schedule an ultrasound and an exam with an obstetrician, perhaps the next time the ship docks back in Florida. I can recommend one and book your appointments, if you would like me to. I'll write you a prescription for vitamins and for the nausea. I want you to come back and see me in a few days so I can monitor your symptoms. And if you choose not to…"

Lily cut her off. "I'm having this baby…I'm sure of that. And if you could arrange those appointments for me, it would be a big help." Her heart told her this was the right decision, with or without Nick.

"I will. Take care, Lily, and I'll see you in a few days. Call the clinic if your symptoms get worse."

The doctor turned and exited, leaving Lily sitting alone in the exam room. She got up and walked over to the small sink in the corner. As she washed her hands and face, she looked in the mirror. Her eyes were just a little bit red now. Willing herself to stop crying, she tried to focus. She had work to get to, and she couldn't look like she was falling apart.

Lily tried to put the doctor's news out of her mind. She could think about it later when she had some time to herself. Of course, she had to figure out what to do, but it would have to wait.

Lily made it to her meeting on time, and it went well. She got some sympathetic looks from her boss and co-workers. Clearly, Rosa had spread the word that she had the flu. If only that was true. Oh well, they could just keep on thinking that for now.

The rest of the day was uneventful until mid-afternoon when Nick came storming into the boutique. He looked tired and a bit disheveled, not the usual look for him. She would have felt sorry for him, if it wasn't for the hard stare he was giving her. *I guess he got my note.*

"Ms. Kingston," he said as he approached her. "May I have a word with you, please? In private."

"Of course, Captain," she said and tried to keep herself calm. She did not want to argue with him, her day had been difficult enough. "Please, come this way."

She led him to the back of the boutique and into the small storage room. It was packed floor to ceiling with boxes of stock, but it was otherwise unoccupied. As soon as they were alone, his anger flashed. "Lily, what are you doing at work? I told you to stay in my cabin and rest."

"Nick," she said. "Calm down. I was feeling better and had a meeting that I couldn't miss. Besides, you were at work, and there was nothing for me to do." She reached up and touched his face with her hands in order to soothe him. It didn't work.

"You were supposed to be sleeping. Not up and

around the ship when you have the flu."

He was looking at her with an intense stare. She flashed to a scene in her mind, one in the near future when she told him she was pregnant. He would be at least this angry or maybe worse. Her composure shattered, and tears rolled down her cheeks. The stress of the past two days was taking its toll. At the sight of her tears, Nick's gaze softened.

"Oh, Lily," he said. "Come here." He took her in his strong arms and stroked her hair. "I'm sorry. I was just so worried about you, and when you weren't in my cabin when I got back, I panicked."

Lily didn't say anything right away. Feeling so warm and safe in his arms, it was impossible to be mad at him. She wiped her face with her hands and took a big gulp of air, breathing in Nick's spicy scent. How many moments like this would they have before he found out the truth about the pregnancy and left her? Well, she wasn't going to tell him today, she had to sort it out for herself first. She looked up at him. He leaned down and placed his lips on hers. They kissed softly at first and then with more intensity.

"It's okay," she murmured when their lips parted. "I've had a long day already, and I'm tired." *And pregnant.* Her hormones were obviously going crazy, which made her laugh and cry at the same time. Hopefully, this was temporary, like for nine months. This realization almost made her start to cry again. Instead, she settled deeper into Nick's embrace.

Nick broke the silence after a few moments. "I'm all finished on the bridge for the day. Crisis averted, thankfully. Why don't you come back with me to my cabin, and we can relax? I think you pushed yourself too hard today."

She didn't want to leave work, despite how she was feeling. Instead, she agreed to meet him in his cabin after her shift. He relented without further comment, probably not wanting to set her off again. Although, he did make her promise to stay at his place tonight, and she had agreed. After all, her days of being in his bed were numbered.

Chapter Seven

In fact, Lily spent every night of the following week in his bed. She did this, hoping she would work up the courage to tell Nick about the pregnancy, but just couldn't bring herself to do it. He had been so caring and attentive to her every need, despite his crazy work schedule. He made sure she ate well and got lots of rest and soon, she was almost feeling like her old self again.

Lily was going to tell him the truth one night before the ship was docking for a week. It was going in for some routine maintenance. They had a whole week off, and she planned to attend her appointments and visit Victoria. Nick had been so busy working, she doubted he had even considered what to do with his time off. Maybe he had to work and oversee the repairs, she wasn't sure. Anyway, it didn't matter. She was positive that after she told him about the baby, he would never want to see her again.

She was trying to relax on a lounge chair on the deck of Nick's suite, waiting for him to come home from his shift. Gorgeous orange, yellow and red hues from the setting sun filled the sky and glinted on the dark blue sea. She would miss this place, but the ache in her heart was all for Nick. For she had fallen in love with him, and she hadn't been able to admit that to herself until now. It was all was about to end, tonight. She stared out at the water, wishing things were different, but it was time to face reality and the twist of fate that had gotten her to this place.

She had already packed up her belongings and placed them in a corner of the bedroom. Nothing could be more embarrassing than hunting for your toothbrush when your boyfriend was kicking you out, so she prepared in advance.

Despite her nerves, she relaxed on the deck and closed her eyes. The soft lull of the ocean was soothing and rocked her into a quiet sleep.

****

Nick found Lily sleeping on the deck after he got back from his shift. The sun had already set, and the moonlight reflected off the water. She was curled up on a deck chair with a blanket around her. He looked at her with tenderness filling his heart to overflowing. She looked so small and peaceful. Walking over to her, he bent down to pick her up. He wanted to bring her inside so she didn't catch a chill. She awakened at his touch and a sad smile crossed her face.

"Hi, gorgeous," he said. "Did you have a good nap? Is everything all right?" He took a seat on the chair next to her and took her hand in his. He sensed an emotion he couldn't quite read in her smile and body language.

"Yes, but, Nick…we need to talk…"

"Sure, but guess what?" He went on, ignoring her tone. He was sure his news would cheer her up and bring that stunning smile he could lose himself in back to her face.

"I just found out I'm off the hook for next week. The engineers are in charge of the maintenance this time around, so we are both free. I want you to come to

St. Petersburg and meet my family. My mom is throwing a dinner for us so I can introduce you to my parents, my brothers Colin and Jon, and my sister Grace. It's going to be great. We can stay at my beachfront condo. What do you think?"

He looked at her, waiting for a response. It was a big step for him. Despite the endless string of women in his past, not very many females were invited to meet the Becket clan. But he was ready to take this monumental step with Lily and hoped she was too. He saw something flash across her face. What was it? Regret? Disappointment? Before he could identify it, her face softened into the familiar smile he loved.

"Sure," she said. "That would be wonderful. I need a few days at the end of the week, to visit Victoria, but I'm all yours until then."

"Perfect. I can't wait to have you all to myself for a whole week. Now what did you want to talk about?"

"Oh, it's nothing really important, and it's getting late. I should get back to my cabin; Alecia must think I have jumped ship."

"Well, she's just going to have to keep thinking that. You're not going anywhere." Without waiting for a response from her, he scooped her up in his arms and carried her from the cool night air into his warm and inviting bed.

****

The next few days were busy for Lily. She hadn't had time to think about her pregnancy and when she was going to tell Nick. She had lost her nerve a few nights ago when he had brought up their trip to St. Petersburg. He had been so excited, and she got caught up in the moment as well. She should have said no.

That was her first instinct. This trip was one-step further into his life, and if she got much deeper, it would only make it that much harder when she lost him.

Well, it was too late for regrets now, Nick had picked her up half an hour ago, and when they exited the ship, he led her to his sapphire blue convertible sports car. He told her how much he missed driving while onboard and he was making up for lost time with a passion as the wind whipped through her hair on the highway.

The scenery blurred by, but Lily didn't care. She sneaked a peek at Nick. He looked happy and relaxed in black cargo shorts and a blue T-shirt with aviator sunglasses hiding his eyes. He caught her looking at him, and she laughed. He grabbed her thigh and looked back at her.

"Having fun?"

"Yes, but you should keep your eyes on the road."

"Well, how can I when you look so hot?"

"Nick, stop. I'm serious."

"So am I. As soon as we get to my place, I'm going to show you how serious I am."

She laughed again, thinking of the nights of pure passion they had spent in each other's arms. Finally feeling better, she could not get enough of him, or he of her. She was clinging to the hope that the ship's doctor had been wrong about her pregnancy and that the Orchard Park doctor would straighten things out.

****

They stopped at a quaint diner for lunch, and Nick was pleased Lily had her appetite back. They ordered burgers, fries, and milkshakes. He loved this place with its red vinyl booths and jukebox playing tunes from the fifties and sixties. His family had come here a lot when he was growing up, and then later as a teenager he came with his friends.

Lily looked happy and carefree in a little white sundress with blue and yellow flowers on it. He wanted to reach out and smooth her windblown hair, but he wouldn't be able to stop there. Instead, he grabbed her hand and asked her about the other night. He sensed something was wrong, but he just couldn't put his finger on it. When he'd tried asking before one thing had led to another, and they hadn't done much talking the rest of the night. That is, unless you count him calling out her name in ecstasy.

Anyway, now was a good time to find out what was troubling her. It was better to do this when they were in public and not thirty feet from his bed.

"Lily, about the other night on my cabin deck. You wanted to tell me something. What was it?"

"Oh that? Don't worry about it. We can discuss it some other time."

"Look, we've been through this before. You're not a good liar. When something is bothering you, I want you to be able to tell me. Why are you holding back?"

"Nick…there is something we need to talk about, but I don't have all the facts yet, so I don't want to get into it. I promise you, I'm okay. It's just…well, nothing we can't discuss when our trip is over. Can you please just trust me and stop worrying?"

Trust. It was a heady concept for Nick. He didn't trust a lot of people, and the list of women outside his family he confided in was virtually non-existent. As he and Lily grew closer, he was beginning to trust her. He might ruin their holiday if he pressed the matter. She was a complicated woman, and he was willing to give her the benefit of the doubt.

"Okay. I suppose it can wait till we get back."

"Good," she said. "Now, let's get going. I don't want to be late to meet your family. I'm already nervous enough."

"Relax. They are going to love you."

****

The Becket house was a breathtaking mansion just outside the city on a corner of the bay. It was a huge sprawling estate with more bedrooms then Lily could count. As she was ushered into the mahogany entryway with fourteen-foot ceilings, she was rendered speechless. Nick's mother Elaine and his father Robert came bustling into view, his mother full of excitement.

"Lily, Nick," Elaine crooned. "We are so happy to see you. Please, come on in. Everyone else is out back."

She enveloped both of them in a warm hug, and Lily shook hands with Nick's father.

He was friendly also, but more reserved. She noticed he was pale and somewhat thin, perhaps from the recent treatments he had undergone for his cancer.

"Very nice to meet you, Lily," said Robert. "Nick doesn't often bring his girlfriends home to his parents, so we were very happy that he wanted us to meet you."

Nick's parents were so welcoming and kind. Meeting them made Lily's heart ache with regret that she would only know them for a very short time before they would no longer want anything to do with her. But she stamped down her erratic emotions and tried to focus.

"Thank you very much," Lily said as she smiled up

at Nick's father. He was very tall, just like his son. Lily was a bit taken aback that Nick didn't show off his former girlfriends to his parents. She was surprised that he didn't have an endless parade of women through this elegant front door. It made her feel special, and a little bit hopeful about their future. It was a small sign, but a good one, nevertheless.

Elaine nodded and agreed with Robert. Then she leaned over and whispered in Lily's ear. "And Nick didn't mention how pretty you are."

Lily blushed in response, unsure of what to say. But she was happy, it was going well so far. Nick's parents were wonderful.

Elaine led everyone through the massive kitchen with its granite countertops and stainless-steel appliances. There were two uniformed people in the space, preparing the food. This was beyond fancy. Her parents had been well off, but not like this.

Then Nick's mother led them outside to the large back deck where the rest of the family was seated on comfortable looking loungers or standing around talking. Nick made quick introductions to his sister Grace and her husband James. They were a friendly couple, and Lily could see from Grace's round belly that she was very pregnant. Why hadn't Nick mentioned this to her? Grace tried to put her arms around Lily, but she couldn't manage. The two women laughed.

"Congratulations. When are you due?"

"Next month," she said and smiled. "It's a girl. James and I are thrilled. We've been married for a year and trying for almost that long. I just can't believe it's finally happening." Grace paused, perhaps unsure if she had said too much. But before Lily could respond she spoke again. "But enough about us. Lily, I'm so happy to meet you. Nick has told me so much about you."

He has? Like what?

"Okay," Nick said. "That's enough out of you, big sister. If you will excuse us, I'm going to take Lily on a tour of the grounds before dinner."

"Good idea," Grace said. "Lily and I will talk later. But in the meantime, have fun."

Nick took Lily's hand and led her down the stairs to the beautiful manicured grounds with native trees and flowers. From there he led her down to the dock, which opened up onto the bay. He pointed out the speedboat and the yacht. He was rambling on about the boats when she interrupted him. "Nick, why didn't you tell me that Grace was pregnant?"

"What? Oh. Well, I just didn't think about it."

"Why? Aren't you excited about being an uncle?" She held her breath, waiting for a response from him.

"Yeah, I guess. But babies aren't really my thing."

Her face fell, and her stomach clenched. It was as she suspected, but hearing him say it, hurt more than she had imagined. She tried to regain her composure. Fortunately, he didn't notice the shift in her emotions.

"Now this, is my thing." He pointed in the distance and led her toward a giant yacht. "C'mon, let's climb aboard."

She followed him without comment. Meeting his family had turned into a huge mistake.

Later, when they got back from the dock, Lily met Nick's younger brother Colin who had a very young woman on his arm and his older brother Jon who was there without a date. They were all very nice, but Lily was feeling overwhelmed. Nick noticed her unease this time and was at her side in an instant.

"Hey," he said with more than a little concern in his voice. "Are you all right?"

"Yes, fine," she lied. "I just can't believe you grew up in this house. It is so exquisite."

"I know, but after so many years, it's just home to me. Don't be intimidated. Can I get you a drink to calm your nerves?"

She almost gave her standard answer of white wine and then stopped herself. She couldn't have alcohol anymore now that she was pregnant. She hoped Nick wouldn't pick up on this change. "I'll just have a ginger ale for now, thank you."

"Coming right up," he said. Then he planted a quick kiss on her cheek and hurried off to the bar.

Lily took in the view of the bay from the lawn. It was stunning. She didn't notice Nick's brother Colin approach her from behind.

"Great view," he said. He was slightly slurring his words. "Wouldn't you say?"

Lily jumped, startled by his approach. "Yes, it certainly is." She looked at Colin and could indeed see the resemblance in all the brothers, but she didn't like the way he was looking at her. He had been drinking.

"So," he said. "You're Nick's flavor of the month, eh?"

"Excuse me?"

"Oh, relax and take it easy, Lily, right? I'm just saying you shouldn't get too comfortable. Nick's not the marrying kind, but I sure hope you've figured that out for yourself. He probably didn't want to hurt your feelings by mentioning it, but the Becket brothers are all about having a good time and not settling down. So my advice is to just enjoy the ride and get off when it stops."

He paused, gave her a pointed look, and then took another swig of his beer. This drunk had shocked her into silence, and she tried in vain to process what he had just said.

Then Nick returned with their drinks. He saw the look on her face. "Everything okay here?"

"Sure brother," said Colin. "The lovely Lily and I were just getting to know each other. Now, if you'll excuse me, I must go and find my date." And with that said he was off.

"Lily. What did my drunk brother say to you?"

"Nothing really," she lied. She now had further proof he was not going to take her news well, and her heart sank. She had made a promise to herself and Nick that she would deal with it after they got back to the ship. "C'mon," she said with a cheery tone she did not feel. "Let's go visit with your parents. I already overheard your mother complaining she doesn't see enough of you."

"Guilty as charged," he said and smiled at her. "Let's go and sit with them."

The rest of the night went well, and she had had no further encounters with Colin. Everyone enjoyed the sumptuous four-course meal served in the enormous dining room. They'd decorated the space in rich brown tones, and the table and chairs were a warm walnut. It was very refined.

Although Lily wasn't very hungry, she tried to sample at least some of the food. Organic salad greens with raspberry vinaigrette was served first. Followed by cream of wild mushroom soup. The main entrée was roasted chicken with scalloped potatoes and vegetables. Crème brûlée was served for dessert. After the meal, she was exhausted. Her frayed nerves were also taking a toll, and it was unsettling to her.

Shortly after dessert, Nick gazed over at her and smiled. "You look tired. Do you want to go?"

"Yes," she said. He took her hand and helped her stand.

"Mother and Father," he said. "Thank you for such a wonderful dinner, but it has been a long day for Lily and me, so we are going to get going."

"Of course, darling," his mother said. "Your father and I will see you out."

The four of them walked back to the stunning foyer, and Lily thanked his parents for their hospitality.

"It was a pleasure to meet you too," Elaine said. "And I hope we will be seeing you again soon."

Not likely. Lily just smiled in response.

Nick kissed his mother and father good-bye then whisked Lily off to his condo on the beach.

****

The rest of the week was like a dream for Nick. He had Lily all to himself, and they did whatever they wanted. No interruptions from his staff or hers and no emergencies for him to attend to. As they sat in the sun on his terrace and took long walks on the beach, they could finally relax. They made love deep into the night and slept away the mornings. He couldn't remember the last time he was this rested.

Although Nick liked his suite on the ship, he loved his beachfront condo even more. A decorator had furnished the place with glass tables and modern-looking sofas and chairs. The masculine look of the space just added to his pride and joy. Even the spare bedroom was done in various shades of brown to suit his style. He had many priceless antiques dotting the tables and fireplace mantel. The place looked like it belonged in a magazine spread for bachelors.

Nick took Lily to all his favorite restaurants in St. Petersburg, and they dined on everything from all-day breakfasts to local seafood. He was relieved she was eating better. His father had lost so much weight during his illness that her lack of appetite in recent weeks had alarmed him.

He wanted to do something special for Lily, to celebrate their time together in St. Petersburg. The idea came to him late one night, while he was watching Lily sleep. They had gone to bed fairly early because she was tired. Since she was getting an extra-long sleep, he figured she wouldn't mind getting up at dawn so he could show her his surprise.

He got up and checked the forecast. The weather looked good for the morning, so he made a phone call and the plan was set. He should head to bed too, so he would be well rested. He snuck back into the bedroom and hovered around Lily.

She looked so relaxed and youthful in his bed. Although she had been trying to hide it from him, something was bothering her, but in sleep she looked so serene and lovely. He ached to wake her up and make love to her, but no, she needed her rest. Besides, they had already had more than a few intimate moments today. He'd quickly found he couldn't get enough of her.

He lay down beside her and closed his eyes. Nick

was feeling content, but thoughts of what was troubling Lily still plagued him. Though, he had kept his word so far and hadn't brought the subject up. He hoped that maybe Lily was just homesick for Victoria and the visit she had planned at the end of the week would lift her spirits. Nick drifted off to sleep with the soothing sounds of the ocean waves coming through the open window and Lily's warm body beside him.

****

When Nick awoke, it was still dark out, but he had to get up and get some things organized. He wanted to let Lily sleep a little longer. He showered and dressed in dark jeans and a black hooded sweatshirt. It was still a bit cold out at this time of day, but it was well worth it to venture out, he was sure. He went into the kitchen and switched on the coffee pot, got out a thermos, and packed up some bagels and pastries for them to have later.

Then he turned on the hall light and went into the master bedroom. Lily was still fast asleep. He walked over and sat beside her on the bed.

"Time to get up, gorgeous," he whispered in her ear and planted a kiss on her forehead. Lily groaned and turned away from the light.

"C'mon. I want to show you something."

"Five more minutes," she mumbled.

"No can do beautiful. I don't want you to miss it, so you have to get up now."

Lily sat up and looked around the room. Her long hair was tangled, and she still had that dreamy-eyed look.

"Nick, its dark out. What is there to see at this hour?"

"Get dressed, and I'll show you. Hurry," he said and lifted her onto her feet. She laughed and sagged against him.

"Okay," she said and stood up straight. "But this better be good. I was planning on sleeping late."

"We can have a nap later, I promise."

She didn't comment, just went into the bathroom and shut the door. Ten minutes later, she emerged dressed like Nick in jeans and a hoody. Her long hair was swept up into a high ponytail, making her look about eighteen with her fresh face. He smiled.

"Let's go," he said taking her hand in his. He grabbed the knapsack with the coffee and breakfast in it, and they set off.

They rode the elevator down in silence. Nick gave Lily a few more minutes to wake up. He led her out of the back of the building and down to the small marina. It housed all of the boats for the condo owners.

Lily was alert now, and she smiled up at Nick. "Are we going for a boat ride?"

"We sure are," he said. "We've shared some beautiful sunsets together, but what I really wanted to show you is a sunrise. They are incredible down by the pier."

He had called down to the marina last night, and they had gotten the boat ready for him. It was his very new, very fast, and very expensive speedboat. They could get there quickly and not miss a minute. It was one of three boats he owned, but he didn't mention that to Lily. She was already intimidated by his wealth, so no need to flaunt it.

She looked at him with wide eyes. "Is this your boat?"

"Oh, this old thing?" he said and laughed. "Yes, now get in. It will get us where we want to go."

"It's beautiful," she said and climbed in. It had luxurious white leather seats, and the instrument panel was all shiny and new. Lily sat down on the passenger side. Nick slid into the captain's chair and smiled at her. "Not half as beautiful as you. Now hang on."

He started the boat, and they headed out onto the bay toward the pier. Nick loved the sound of the engine roaring and the fresh scent of the spraying salt water.

They reached the pier a few minutes before sunrise. Nick docked the boat and poured some coffee for them. He saw a shiver pass over Lily, so he moved closer to her and wrapped her in a heavy wool blanket he kept on the boat.

"Wait for it," he said as he breathed into the cool air. Suddenly, the sky lightened, and the huge orange and yellow sphere of the sun became visible.

"Oh, Nick," Lily said and looked mesmerized by the sight. "This is so amazing. I've actually never seen a sunrise. I'm not exactly a morning person, but it was worth getting up so early. This is a gorgeous sight."

He smiled down at her. It was indeed a stunning sight. The sky was filling with light, and there were whispers of clouds on the horizon. The boat bobbing up and down in the water was calming. Nick had been out here countless times, alone. He sometimes brought the boat out here to think, reflect, and make important decisions, but he hadn't had a girl with him, until now. Before he'd met Lily, he hadn't wanted to. She had changed everything. She had changed him.

The sun was now climbing higher in the sky. It had risen, and it was going to be a splendid day. She looked up into his eyes. Her expression showed a joy and happiness he hadn't seen in any of the other girls he had dated.

"Nick," she whispered. He leaned over to take his hand in hers. "You have shown me so many wonderful things, and for that I will be forever grateful."

Nick paused, confused at the tone of her voice. It was as if she was saying good-bye. But that couldn't be, could it? Since he didn't want to ruin this otherwise perfect moment, he stayed silent. Instead of responding to her statement, he leaned down and kissed her cheek.

He ran little kisses down her face until he got to her lips. There he deepened the kiss and slid his tongue into her mouth. He tasted coffee, and his whole body responded to their contact. They stayed like this for a very long time before he broke it off. She was still shivering, so he wanted to get her back to the condo and into his bed.

"Let's head back," he said, with a brightness in his tone, he just didn't feel. "You're cold, and I want to get you home."

Lily laughed and snuggled closer. "Well, it was worth it, even if this morning is freezing."

Despite the heat of their embrace and her carefree laugh, Nick noticed a distance between them. Once they were back on the ship, she would have to tell him what was going on. He wouldn't let this go on much longer and tried not to let his imagination run wild, but with her recent illness and his father's diagnosis in the back of his mind, he was a little more than concerned. He just had to hope everything would turn out all right.

****

The end of the week came much too fast for Nick.

He had tried in vain to get Lily to allow him to come to Orchard Park with her, but she insisted on going alone. As it turned out, it was for the best, since he had some meetings to attend at Caribbean Paradise headquarters. Although his dad had looked better on this visit, Nick wanted to get the straight facts from his siblings about his father's health, so he had set up a meeting with everyone. He was always the last to know things because he was so busy, but he wanted to try to stay on top of what was going on. He had also wanted to play a few rounds of golf with his brothers.

Besides, it would be too depressing sitting in his condo all by himself with images of Lily everywhere. They had made great use of the space, most of the time with their clothes off. He smiled at the memories. It was just her reaction to the sunrise that still bothered him. She had loved it, but she was distant and sad, if only for a fleeting moment.

Lily and Nick had planned to meet back on the ship on Saturday evening after they had set sail again. It would be a busy working day for both of them, but they were already going to be spending two days apart, and that was more than enough for Nick.

He rented her a practical SUV for the trip to Orchard Park. No sports cars for her, they were too dangerous. He lingered next to the car. She was sitting in the driver's seat, all packed up and ready to go, but he was trying to steal a few more minutes with her.

"Are you sure you have to leave so early?" he asked her. "Come back up to the condo for a few hours, and I'll make you forget all about going to Orchard Park."

She laughed. "Nick, you know I have to get going.

Victoria is expecting me, and you have a golf date with your brothers."

"Oh that can be canceled for you," he said with a wave of his hand.

"No," she said. "As much as I've had the most fantastic time, my best friend is waiting, and it's been ages since I saw her. So give me a kiss, and I'll be on my way."

"Of course," he said without further argument. He leaned down to touch her soft full lips with his. He slid his tongue into her mouth and tasted her minty toothpaste. He pulled back and took a long look at her angelic face. "Drive safe, honey, and call me when you get there."

"I will. Good luck with your game. Talk soon."

And then she was off, driving down the winding road away from him. He stared after the car. This woman had him mesmerized with her body and soul, and it was too late to turn back now. He could easily admit that to himself now, but how could he explain that to her?

Chapter Eight

Nick shook off his wayward thoughts and made his way over to the car. He hopped in and drove the short distance to the private golf club that all the Becket men belonged to.

He met his brother Jon in the lobby, and they exchanged a quick hug. Jon was Nick's baby brother. Ever since they were kids, Nick had always been a bit overprotective of Jon. He looked like Nick with his bright blue eyes, but he kept his light blond hair longer and brushed back from his face. There was eight years between them and at twenty-seven, Jon was the youngest in the family. Despite this, he had a personality and way about him that made him appear older than his calendar years.

"Hey man," Jon said. "How are you doing?"

"Good, really good. Where's Colin?"

"He couldn't make it. Something about a hot blonde still in his bed. Go figure."

Nick smiled at his brother's comment. He found he didn't miss those days at all. He liked waking up to Lily by his side, not some woman whose name he couldn't remember.

"That's okay. We have a lot to catch up on without hearing about Colin's latest conquests. I know you are going through a rough time right now, and we didn't get a chance to catch up at Mom and Dad's." Nick was referring to Jon's recent break up with his long-time girlfriend.

"Lots of time for catching up later," Jon said. "First, I'm going to kick your ass on the golf course."

"Oh, you think so, do you? Well game on, brother, let's go."

To Nick's dismay, his brother did beat him badly. He just couldn't focus. Thoughts of Lily were clouding his mind, but the truth was, he didn't mind losing to Jon. His brother had been hitting the course hard the last few weeks, and his game was much improved.

They put their gear away and met up for lunch at the club's restaurant on the patio.

"So," Jon said when they were seated and sharing a pitcher of beer. "I enjoyed meeting Lily. It looks like she's having a good effect on you. No more one night stands?"

"No, I think those days are over. She's unlike any other woman I've dated. I can't stop thinking about her. Like today, she's off to her girlfriend's for the night, and I almost can't stand to be away from her."

"Is it lust? Or love?" Jon said with an arched eyebrow.

"Lust for sure," Nick said and laughed. "But also something more. I just can't figure it out, at least not yet."

"Well, my big brother is finally acting his age. But seriously, listen to me. If she is the one for you Nick, don't let her get away."

"Thanks for the advice, baby brother. But I don't think she's going anywhere."

"Good. Because let me tell you, I can't believe I let Kristen go."

Nick gave his brother a sympathetic look. Kristen and Jon had been dating for years, but she was ready to settle down and Jon wasn't. By the time Jon had made up his mind about marrying her, she had already moved on and he had lost her. It had been very difficult for him, and he was taking it hard. Nick was hopeful he would meet someone new soon.

"I'm really sorry about what happened. What are your plans now?"

"Oh, just to become a workaholic and wallow in my misery."

Nick frowned and made an attempt to cheer him up. "C'mon. You already work too hard. Any news on the dating scene?"

"I'm just not ready, but thanks for asking. Now let's order lunch, I'm starved."

"Okay," Nick said without further comment. They ordered sandwiches, and the conversation flowed about work and family. But Jon's advice about Lily kept coming back to him, and he still didn't know exactly what to make of it.

****

Lily cried all the way to the Orchard Park Medical Center. Victoria was meeting her there for her appointment. She had just experienced a wonderful few days with Nick, but she was pretty sure she had shared his bed for the last time. His condo was no place to raise a baby, despite its richness. All that glass and chrome was not somewhere any child should live.

Of course, he had never tried to keep his wealth a secret, but his family and home had overwhelmed her. Despite this, she still didn't want any of his money. Lily would find a way to raise the baby on her own. She had no idea how, but she would work it out. A clean break would be better for everyone.

She was a complete wreck when she pulled into the parking lot and saw Victoria waiting for her. She came over and wrapped Lily in a warm hug. This just made her cry harder.

"Oh, Lily," she soothed. "Come now, we've been through much worse than this, and you know you have my complete support. Let's go inside and get you registered with the nurse."

"All right," Lily said and allowed Victoria to guide her.

They went into the clinic, and Lily had the prescribed tests and met with her obstetrician. The doctor confirmed that she was about three months along, and everything was fine. She indicated she was worried about Lily's state of mind, but Victoria assured the doctor she would take care of her.

After the appointment, they drove back to Victoria's house, and she fixed lunch. Tom had taken the twins to his mother's for the night, so they had some time alone. Lily refused to eat, claiming she was not hungry.

"Lily. You have to eat. You can't just think about yourself anymore. You have a precious life growing inside you, and you must take care of her or him."

Victoria was right of course; it was just such a big adjustment for Lily. She had to get used to thinking about the baby. The baby. This made her smile as she had hoped to have children one day, but not like this, single and alone. Her body ached for Nick, his tender touch, his warm embrace. Well, she just had to get used to this new reality because soon, he wasn't going to be there.

"You're right," she said. "Let's have some lunch. I'm sorry I'm such a mess. I just can't get used to the idea I'm pregnant."

"I know. It's a huge step for you, but you didn't get into this situation by yourself. Have you had a chance to tell Nick yet?"

"No," she said and sighed. "I've almost told him a few times, but at the last second I got scared and didn't mention it. I just don't want to lose him. He doesn't want a baby. He barely wanted a steady girlfriend until I came along. Nick talks about settling down someday, but I just can't see it. He's such a free spirit."

"Well, free spirit or not, you have to talk to him as soon as you get back. Maybe he will surprise you. Stranger things have happened."

"I don't think so, but I am going to tell him, tomorrow night. I promise. He has a right to know. I'm sure he will break up with me, though."

"Lily, whatever happens when you tell him, I want you to know you can depend on me to help you, always. In fact, I was going to suggest you come and stay in the spare bedroom here, once you take your leave from the cruise line."

"Victoria, no. I can't impose on you, Tom, and the twins."

"Nonsense. I've already talked to Tom and he agrees, and the twins adore you. It's not forever, just until you get back on your feet after you have the baby. Lily, you are my best friend, and if friends can't help each other out during difficult times, what are they good for? You would do the same if the roles were reversed, I know it."

"Well, okay, thank you so much. I don't know how I can ever repay you."

"You can start by eating…" Victoria said and smiled. The two women embraced, and Lily's spirits were lifted. It was a great relief to be able to talk to someone. Victoria was a true friend and having raised two babies at once, she was full of experience.

The two women shared a fun evening together, laughing and talking, just like old times. They sat on Victoria's back deck for hours, catching up, and then watched a movie on television. Lily was staying in Victoria's spacious spare room, and it was as close to home as she had been in a long time.

She called Nick, and they chatted for a few moments about their respective days. She tried to keep the conversation light and avoided all mention of the real reason for her visit. As they talked, Lily listened to the sound of his voice, so smooth and deep. She loved this and everything about him, but he didn't love her back. He liked her sure, but it just wasn't enough to make it work. Well, tomorrow he would know everything, and she'd better get used to sleeping alone.

Saturday was a hectic day for Lily. After an early breakfast with Victoria, she drove back to Port Canaveral. From there, she boarded the ship and spent the day getting the boutique ready for customers. On her lunch break, she had planned to take a few minutes to call Nick, but in the end she didn't. She didn't want to lose her nerve, again. She was just going to show up at his cabin after work and tell him everything.

The ship sailed on time, and they were well under way by seven o'clock. Lily figured Nick would be in his suite by then. She went back to her cabin to unpack and spend a few minutes with her roommate. Alecia had a wonderful trip back to Jamaica and made Lily promise she would visit her there one day. Lily said she would love to.

She changed out of her work uniform and into jeans and a soft green hoody she'd had for ages. Best to be as comfortable as possible when your boyfriend dumps you. Anyway, she was trying to make plans for her future, a future without Nick. It was difficult, but she was beginning to face reality.

She took the long route up to his suite and marveled at the beauty of the ship. Even months after she first boarded and had seen it a hundred times, it was still fresh to her at every encounter. It was such a magnificent vessel, and she would miss it. However, she couldn't raise a baby while working on a cruise line. That was out of the question.

She knocked on Nick's door at twenty minutes past seven. The door burst open, and Nick was standing there, dressed in a towel, his blond hair still wet from his recent shower. He grabbed her arm and tugged her inside. The door slammed shut behind her. Then she was up against the back of it in an instant, his body pressed against hers. His hard muscles were rigid, and he was already aroused by their contact. He leaned down and kissed her. She could smell the scent of his spicy aftershave. And as she tasted the minty flavor of his toothpaste, she sighed and almost lost her nerve.

"Hi, beautiful," he whispered in her ear. "I missed you. You're right on time, but you're way overdressed. Let me take care of that for you."

Lily almost melted into a puddle in his arms. She would have loved nothing better than to indulge him and herself for that matter, but she just couldn't. Not today. He had to know the truth, and if she stayed in his embrace any longer, she wouldn't go through with it.

"Nick," she said and tried to keep the mood light, for now. "I missed you too, but we really need to talk."

"Later…" he murmured and trailed kisses down the side of her neck as he reached for the zipper on her sweatshirt.

She almost gave in, but remembered her promise to Victoria and the life growing inside her. Nick's baby. And he didn't have a clue.

"No, Nick, now." She tried to extricate herself from him.

He looked into her eyes and saw her serious expression. Then he backed up a step.

"Honey, what's wrong? Did something happen in Orchard Park? You didn't mention anything on the phone."

"Yes and no," she said. "Why don't you put some clothes on, and I'll meet you out on the deck."

He looked down as if momentarily confused and then he recovered some composure. "Sure. Be right back. Help yourself to a drink. We can order dinner whenever you are hungry."

"Fine," she said. She had never spoken to him in such a harsh tone. She reserved this businesslike voice for her employees, not her lover. Fortunately, he didn't comment, he just disappeared into the bedroom.

She poured herself a glass of water for something to do and walked out onto the terrace. The view was breathtaking. The port was a pinpoint in the distance and dusk was beginning to set in. Indigo and violet hues colored the sky. The rush of the water was a soothing sound, and she remembered the many nights she had spent out here with Nick, dining, dancing, and just being together. She would miss this place something fierce, but not half as much as she would miss Nick. Her eyes filled with tears as she tried to focus on the task at hand, but it was too late.

Nick had seen her. He had been watching her from the doorway, and he stood with a confused and troubled look on his face. He was dressed in navy track pants and a white T-shirt. The shirt showed off his glowing tan, and his biceps were bulging from his clenched fists. His hair was spiked, as if he had been running his hands through it. She could tell he knew she didn't have good news, but she was sure he would never guess what it was.

"Lily," he called to her. "Come inside and let's sit down. It's getting too cold out here."

She lingered on the deck, not wanting to move, but it was probably better to talk in the cabin. Lily nodded at him and then followed him through the glass doors. Taking a seat on the luxurious black leather sofa, she looked everywhere but at him. He sat down beside her and took her hand. He lifted her chin with his fingers and forced her to look deep into his eyes. They were full of concern.

"Tell me what's going on...I'm frantic with worry. Are you sick again?"

She paused, not knowing how to respond. Nick was hypersensitive to illness, what with his father's cancer diagnosis. Lily was just going to be honest with him and tell it to him straight just like the doctor had done to her.

"No, Nick, I'm not sick. I'm pregnant."

"You're what?" He let go of her hand and stared at her with a look of horror and disbelief etched on his gorgeous face.

She said it again, just in case he hadn't actually heard her, although she was sure he had.

"No, that's not possible. We always used protection. Are you sure it's mine?"

The words stung her, but she suspected that he would have a hard time accepting it. "Yes, Nick. The baby is yours. I haven't been with anyone but you, since my divorce. And we didn't always use protection, not the first night." And then she couldn't help herself by getting her own jab in. "And I'm not the one with the endless string of lovers, that's your style."

Nick looked confused for a moment, and Lily assumed he was trying to think back to their first night together. Then his confusion turned to anger.

"For your information, Lily Kingston, ever since the night we met I haven't been with any other women. Nevertheless, I want a paternity test. If you think you are going to get at my money without proving I'm the father, you're dead wrong."

"You can get whatever test you want, Nick," she retorted. "It's not going to make a difference. And furthermore, you can keep your millions all to yourself. I don't want any of it!"

"What?"

Lily was getting tired of repeating herself. "I said, I don't want your money or anything else from you for that matter. And I think it's time for me to go." She got up and headed for the door. It was over and done with. She was relieved, but her heart ached more right now than it ever had before.

Lily had told him what she came here to say, and if she stayed any longer, their argument would only get worse. This was the end of their relationship. She had to move on. Time heals all wounds; her mother had always said. She didn't know why that came to mind. Well, she would have lots of time in the coming days, alone.

"Lily wait," Nick said as he walked toward her. "I…"

Lily cut him off. "Nick, I think we've said all there is to say. I'm pregnant. It's not something either of us planned, but it is reality. You don't have any interest in being a father or settling down. If I had any doubts about that, my conversation with your brother Colin and your behavior tonight made it clear to me. Good-bye." And then she was gone, slamming the door behind her.

****

Nick stood in stunned silence staring at the closed door. He wanted Lily to come back, but he had no idea what he would say to her if she did. *Me, Nicholas Becket, a dad?* That idea was incomprehensible to him. It was not on his radar, and he didn't know if it would ever be.

He was just beginning to be a decent boyfriend to Lily, and that was a pretty foreign concept for him in itself. He sighed and walked over to the mini bar. He took a couple shots of tequila and sat down on his couch. What should he do? What was she going to do? He had been so concerned about this impacting his life, that he hadn't given Lily or the baby a second thought.

Was she okay? Was it a boy or a girl? His head was beginning to clear, the alcohol was slowing down his racing mind. He took a few more shots, since the first two worked so well. He had to be up early the next day for work, but he didn't care.

And what was that off handed comment about Colin? He would have to find out about that later, and he should probably call his lawyer. Nick had some friends who had gotten themselves involved with women who were only after their money with disastrous consequences. He wasn't going to let that happen to him. Even though he believed Lily when she said she didn't want support, things could change, and he didn't want to be unprepared.

As he downed his fifth tequila, or was it his sixth, he imagined what life would be like without Lily. She had broken it off with him before he had the chance to say much of anything. But he almost couldn't blame her. What he had said was uncalled for, and he had acted like a real jerk. He had accused her of sleeping around. What had he been thinking? She had spent almost every night over the last month in his bed.

He just really didn't want to accept the fact that he had had a part in creating a new life. One that needed extraordinary care and was a huge responsibility. Although he had been raised well by loving parents, he was well aware of the fact that it took great sacrifice and a lifestyle he just couldn't imagine for himself.

He didn't know what else to do, so he grabbed the bottle of tequila and took a swig. Forget about the shot glass. Forget about all of this. He was hoping it was all just a bad dream, and he would wake up any minute with Lily asleep beside him. He began to feel dizzy. He hadn't had dinner, and the alcohol was hitting him hard. *Good. I'll just pass out, and this terrible nightmare will be over.*

He lay down on the couch and closed his eyes. Nick couldn't face his room tonight. Thinking about his big cold bed without her made him shudder with dread. As he drifted off to sleep, he found himself talking to the empty room. "I love you, Lily Kingston, but I don't think I can ever tell you now."

****

Lily wandered around the ship for hours before returning to her cabin. She visited all of the places she had loved most on the ship. The pool area, the lounge, the skating rink, and even the casino where she had watched Nick play blackjack. She had a sad smile on her face as she watched all the happy passengers. This place was paradise. She walked the perimeter of the ship, soaking in the cool breeze from the ocean and tasting the salty spray, for what could be the last time.

She had made a decision, long before she went to see Nick tonight. Lily was going to leave the ship as soon as possible. There was no point in staying here any longer than she had to. She had a lot of work to do to put her life back together, and she needed to get started. It was the right decision. But standing out here, leaning on the railing of the ship, she realized she would miss this place. It was where she had found freedom from her past, where she had fallen in love. Now it was the place where love had been lost, and it was time to move on.

She wandered back to her cabin, exhausted from the stress of the day and her marathon walk around the ship. Lily wanted to fall into bed and forget this terrible day. Usually Alecia was out with her friends, but when Lily got back, she was in their cabin reading.

"Hey, girl," Alecia called when she saw Lily. "How's it going?"

"I'm okay, I guess."

"Lily, what's wrong?" Alecia had a concerned look on her face. She put down her book and rushed over to Lily's side.

Lily didn't want to get into the details of her evening with Alecia. After all, she had tried to warn her about Nick the first day on the ship, and she hadn't listened. However, Alecia was a good roommate, and she needed someone to talk to.

"Nick and I broke up," she said. Then her eyes filled with tears and spilled down her cheeks.

"Oh, Lily, I'm so sorry." Alecia said as she enveloped Lily in a big hug. "Do you want to talk about it?"

"Well, I guess I might as well tell you, since I'll be leaving soon."

"Leaving? Why would you leave? If that playboy told you to abandon ship, I'm going to march up to his cabin right now and give him a piece of my mind."

Lily laughed through her tears. Alecia was a good friend. She was glad she got a chance to talk to her, instead of her earlier plan to sneak off without saying good-bye.

"No, it's nothing like that, but thank you. I really appreciate you being on my side."

"Always, girlfriend, always. Now come sit down and tell me the whole story."

Alecia led Lily over to her bed, and the two women sat down. Lily could see the concern on Alecia's face, and she loved her for it. She didn't know where to begin, so she just started with her big news.

"I'm pregnant, and I told Nick tonight."

"Wow. I'm guessing Nick didn't take the news well."

"Not at all. Anyway, I need to sort out a million things before the baby is born, so I think I'm going to leave the ship soon."

"Well, I will miss you, Lily, but if you need anything, let me know. I want you to steer clear of Nicholas Becket. I think he has done enough damage."

"Yes, you're probably right." Alecia was only trying to help her, but it was almost tearing her apart knowing she wouldn't see Nick again.

"Now," Alecia said. "You look dead on your feet, girl. Let's go to bed and get a good night's sleep. I can help you with whatever plans you need to make in the morning."

"Thank you, Alecia. You are a wonderful friend."

"You don't have to thank me, Lily. We girls have to look out for each other. Now off to bed with you."

The two women exchanged another hug, and Lily changed into her pajamas and climbed into her bunk. She was very tired but couldn't fall asleep. Lily kept picturing Nick's face. His breathtaking smile and gorgeous blue eyes. As she cried herself to sleep that night, she put this endless day where it belonged, in the past.

Chapter Nine

To say that Nick was difficult to get along with for the next few days was a huge understatement. He had a massive hangover the next morning and every morning thereafter. Apparently, drinking an entire bottle of tequila, rum, or whatever he had on hand each night wasn't such a great idea after all. He couldn't think of anything else that would numb the pain of loss in his heart the way alcohol did. Even if it was temporary and ill-advised.

He was late for his shifts, looked about as bad as he felt, and spent most of his days barking orders at anyone and everyone who got in his way. After this had been going on for several days, his friend and second-in-command Daniel cornered him in the Captain's Lounge one morning. Nick poured them both a cup of strong black coffee, even though he doubted it would improve his mood, and the two men sat down in comfortable club leather chairs.

"Nick, man, what is up with you?" Daniel asked. "Me and most of the senior staff are really worried about you. You just aren't yourself lately. Hey, it's gotten so bad that some of the engineers are threatening to quit, and I don't have to tell you, that would be a huge disaster mid-voyage. What gives?"

Although he was Nick's subordinate, they were good enough friends that Nick wasn't too surprised about his concern. Nick sighed and tried to decide whether to shrug off Daniel's questions or be honest with him. He *was* a bear to be around lately. Yelling at his staff for minor infractions and flying off the handle at the smallest setback was not his usual way of commanding the ship. He wouldn't have made it this far, if that had been the case. He wanted to be upfront with Daniel, he could trust him. Daniel had already suspected his involvement with Lily, but he hadn't mentioned it. He had remained a faithful first officer to Nick.

"I've been dating this girl," Nick said.

"Yeah, Lily," he said. "I know you were trying to keep it under wraps, but you know how cruise line gossip goes. You used to be the life of the party and now..."

Nick was dismayed that everyone was talking about them. Not that it was a secret, per se, but now that things had turned out badly, everyone would know that too. Despite this revelation, Nick continued, "Anyway, yes things were going well, and I was getting comfortable being a one woman man. I know, that sounds crazy for me."

"No, it doesn't. I had faith that you would settle down. You just had to find the right girl to do that with. Y'know, when Jane and I started dating, we had some pretty big ups and downs. But look at us now, we're so happy."

Nick gave his friend a sad smile. Daniel was just trying to cheer him up, but the minor arguments he'd had with his girlfriend Jane were nothing compared to what he was going through with Lily. "Yeah, well, things were going great. Then last week she told me she was pregnant and broke up with me."

"Ouch," Daniel said. "That's harsh man, I'm really sorry. What are you going to do?"

"I don't know." Nick leaned over and put his head in his hands. The constant headache he'd been battling for days intensified. "So far I've done nothing but get drunk and yell at my employees. That's not working out too well for me. What would you do, if Jane told you she was having your baby?"

"I would marry her, of course. No other option for me. I love her, man. She's my whole world. Do you feel that way about Lily?"

"I'm not sure. I care about her. But her and a baby? It's just too much." Nick let out a long exhale and raked a hand through his already messy hair.

"Why don't you give it some time? Talk to her and try to work something out. It is a big step all at once, but you're not a kid anymore. Heck, we're almost middle aged."

Nick laughed for the first time in days. Daniel was joking of course, but also right. He needed a bit more time to sort out his feelings, and then he would talk to Lily.

"Thanks, Daniel. For someone who doesn't talk much, you give really good advice." He had always been the quiet friend, but he always managed to tell him what he needed to hear.

"No problem, anytime. And Nick, about the staff?"

"Yeah, I'll lighten up, I promise."

"Great. Let's get back to work."

Nick felt better after his talk with Daniel, better than he had in days. It was time to face Lily again…soon.

****

Two days later, when the ship was getting ready to dock, Nick went to see Lily. He was heartsick being alone and a part of himself was missing without her. They had to find a way to make it work.

He was planning to take her to a quiet but elegant Greek restaurant in the Cape. They would talk and decide what to do, together. He was ready to step up and take responsibility, an epic move for him. Because if he didn't, he would risk losing her forever, and he wasn't willing to entertain those thoughts.

Nick checked her schedule and discovered that she had the day off, since the boutique was closed. He headed down to her cabin early to catch her before she left for the day. He hoped she didn't have other plans, but he didn't know for sure. They had been completely out of contact for almost five days, but it was like an eternity to Nick.

He was dressed in casual cargo pants and a navy shirt. A hot shower and a shave, made him feel better; these were things he had definitely neglected lately. He had also laid off the booze for the past few days, so his bloodshot eyes were back to their brilliant blue.

He knocked on Lily's cabin door, feeling nervous and not sure what to say. Alecia opened the door and frowned at him but was respectful.

"Good Morning, Captain," she said. "How can I help you?"

He could sense the anger in her tone. This was not good. Lily had probably told her everything. Well, he wasn't here to speak to her, but he didn't see Lily in the room behind her. He wasn't sure how much information Alecia would share with him.

"I want to see Lily. Is she here?"

"Why don't you come inside, Captain?"

Nick stepped into the small space, and Alecia shut the door behind him. He was instantly claustrophobic as the walls closed in on him, and his stomach churned with dread.

"She's not here." Alecia glared at him.

He winced at her tone. She was no longer trying to hide her dislike for him.

"Where is she?" he said. He was beginning to lose his patience with her.

"She left."

"What do you mean she left? The ship hasn't even docked yet."

"She went home two days ago, Nick." She had dismissed her earlier formality with him. "She got off the boat in St. Thomas and flew back to Florida. She wasn't feeling well, and you were nowhere to be found. I took her to the airport myself, and now you finally show up, wanting what? To hurl more accusations at her? To make her feel worse than she already does?"

"No, I just wanted to talk to her. I didn't realize she would leave."

"Well, she did. And now you can too. Get out." She flung open the door and gestured for him to step outside. He did so without comment, and she slammed the door in his face.

Normally, he wouldn't allow a subordinate to speak to him like that, but the mixture of shock and the cold truth hit him hard. Alecia had been a good friend to Lily. She had been there for her when he was passed out drunk in his cabin, denying reality. Lily gone, again? For good this time? No, he wouldn't let this happen. He hated that he couldn't just abandon ship and run after her. If, no, when he did track her down, would she even talk to him? Well, there was only one way to find out.

****

As Lily sat staring out the window in her office, she didn't notice the beautiful late fall day outside her window. She was lost in the past. *How did I end up back here?* Of course, the answer to that was clear, but it somehow amazed her how her life had turned out.

Lily had been home for three weeks now. If you called living in Victoria's spare room home. It was comforting, nonetheless, and she would get her own place eventually. She just needed some time to work things out. Victoria and Tom had been so sweet to her, giving her space when she needed it or trying to cheer her up when she was down.

At least she had stopped dissolving into tears every five minutes. It was progress. Baby steps, literally. The twins were helping as well. You couldn't stay miserable surrounded by those two happy faces.

Lily had been working on her finances. She had gotten quite good managing on her own after her divorce, she just needed to get back at it. When she went to see Marguerite, her former boss at the insurance company, she had been thrilled to see her. She gave Lily her old job back right on the spot. The latest receptionist her supervisor hired had just been let go. No one was working out, so her timing was perfect. Lily was well aware how difficult Marguerite was to get along with, so she wasn't too surprised.

She had started back to work the previous day, and in some ways, it was like she hadn't left. But it was what she was used to, and she needed the money. In April, when the baby was due, she would have enough saved to take a short leave of absence when she gave birth. That realization was comforting.

She was getting excited about the baby. Lily had always wanted children but never imagined she would have one on her own. Victoria was so supportive; she was beginning to be hopeful. They had gone shopping last week and picked out some clothes. Lily was astounded about how small and delicate they were, and Victoria had just smiled at her and relished in her fascination. Victoria was trying to be positive for Lily despite the unforeseen circumstances that had brought her back to Orchard Park, and she loved her for that.

Lily had been to see the doctor last week. Everything was going well with the pregnancy. She was almost four months along. She had gained a bit of weight and had a small baby bump, but it made her smile. Her baby, growing inside her. The nausea had pretty much disappeared too, which was a relief.

She had another ultrasound three days earlier, and the doctor had told her she was having a boy. She had had a bittersweet moment then, wishing Nick had been there with her to hear he was having a son. It was at moments like this her heart still ached for him, and she longed to be in his strong protective arms again. She was trying to be realistic about the situation. In fact, she was pretty sure he was back to his partying bachelor days. She hadn't had any contact with him since she left him standing at his cabin door almost a month ago. By now, she didn't expect to.

She was still in touch with Alecia, who asked Lily how she was doing and never mentioned Nick. Lily didn't have the heart to ask her if she had seen him. They were both moving on with their separate lives. All in all, it was for the best.

The fax machine whirred to life and brought her back into the present moment. She hoped it was the office supply company confirming her order. She walked across the small space. As she pulled the papers from the machine, she noticed it was merely an advertisement.

"Is everything all right, dear?" came a voice from the other side of the room. It was Marguerite, her supervisor. She'd better not be caught daydreaming again. Lily had already been spoken to this week about not paying enough attention to detail. She had made a mistake and ordered the wrong type of printer paper. For that she had gotten a long lecture, which would have had most employees running for the nearest exit. In fact, her boss had already gone through two assistants in the short time she had been away, but Lily put up with it because she needed this job, now more than ever.

"Yes, everything is fine. I was waiting for the confirmation of our office supply order, but it was just some ads coming through."

"Well, all right then," she said. "Time to get back to work." Just then Marguerite's phone rang, and she rushed into her small office adjacent to Lily's work area to answer the call.

Her supervisor's attitude made Lily wonder why they had hired her back in the first place. She couldn't make a move without Marguerite looking over her shoulder, and she always double checked her work. But she couldn't afford to lose her job now, especially since she didn't want any support from Nick. With her due date fast approaching, she was lucky to have a job at all, and with that depressing fact clear in her mind, she sighed and got on with her day.

After work, Lily was out running some errands, when she got a text from Victoria. She wanted to meet her at their favorite café in town. She responded saying she would, but if Victoria was busy today, which she usually was, they could go out some other time. Victoria had been trying to get Lily out of the house as much as possible, and Lily loved her dearly for it, but she didn't want Victoria neglecting her work or the kids for her. She was back on her feet and didn't need a babysitter.

Victoria insisted, saying she was all caught up. They agreed to meet in half an hour. She had just enough time for to go to the bank and then walk the few blocks to the café. It was a cozy little place with comfortable chairs and a huge fireplace that took up one wall. Lily had spent hours there, curled up in one of the overstuffed chairs, sipping her tea, reading the paper, or planning out her new life. A new life for her and her precious baby boy.

The cruise ship had been a fun and exciting experience, but Lily wouldn't have done it forever, even if she hadn't gotten pregnant. She liked living in a small town and thought it was a great place to raise a baby. The cramped quarters she shared with Alecia had at times, been overwhelming small. Of course, Nick's cabin had been spacious, and she had spent most of her time with him.

Nick. Why did he pop into her head at the strangest times? She supposed she would always have a soft spot for him, after all he was the father of her child, whether he acknowledged him or not. Although, she found she was thinking of him less and considered that a good sign.

She reached the café twenty minutes later. Bob, the barista, was there to greet her by name when she visited in the late afternoon. He was an older man, a grandfather in fact who said he loved coffee so much he took a part time job here after retirement. He got Lily's herbal tea ready for her as soon as he saw her walk in.

They chatted for a few minutes about the colder weather and the upcoming Thanksgiving holiday. She was spending it with Victoria and Tom and going to help with the cooking. It was the least she could do. She looked around and didn't see Victoria yet, so she curled up in one of the chairs by the fire and pulled out a book to read while she waited. She sipped the herbal brew and stared at the fire. It was peaceful here, so she closed her eyes for a moment to relax after her stressful day at the office.

****

Ever since Nick found out Lily had left the ship, he'd started making plans. They were drastic, life altering plans, but each decision he made was right. Right for him, Lily, and their baby.

As soon as the ship docked, Nick pulled his senior staff aside for an important meeting. He told them he was resigning as captain of the ship and was promoting Daniel to take his place. Mark, his second officer was promoted to first officer, and Nick had contacted headquarters to hire a replacement for Mark. The staff was surprised by this turn of events, but they wished Nick well on his future endeavors.

After this monumental announcement, he met up with Daniel to have a private conversation.

"Hey, Nick. Are you sure you want to do this?"

"Yes, I'm sure."

"Because if you want to change your mind and continue to be captain, that's cool with me. I mean, I would love the promotion of course. And I feel I am qualified for the job. It's just, well this seems drastic and out of character for you."

"Daniel," Nick said. "You are a true friend, and I appreciate your concern. But really, this is what I want. I have to move on with my life if I ever want to get Lily back, of that I'm certain."

"Okay. You've always had good judgement, so I'm sure this time is no exception. Hey, man, I wish you the best of luck and keep in touch."

"I will," said Nick. "And I'm counting on you to take care of the Moonlight Queen. Are you up for it?"

"Yes, One hundred percent. I won't let you down, Captain."

Nick breathed out a sigh of relief. The two men embraced, and then Nick said he had to be on his way. With that task completed, he packed up his belongings and disembarked from the ship for the last time.

On the drive to St. Petersburg, he went over everything he needed to do. He met with his decorator and went over the changes he wanted. She was a bit hesitant at first, but he insisted and she agreed. He was her highest paying customer, so she couldn't afford to lose him. She reported that all the changes could be completed in about two weeks. Nick wanted them sooner, but he was asking a lot, so he didn't push it.

Next, he went to Caribbean Paradise headquarters

to meet with his father. He was seated at his desk, looking well. Nick was pleased. His father was feeling better and back to work a few times a week, but Nick hoped he wasn't overdoing it. When Nick entered his office, Robert got up and came over to give him a hug.

"Hello, son," he said. "How are you doing?"

"I'm doing well, Dad. How are you?"

"Good, thanks for asking. I hear you have been making some changes. Do you want to talk about it?"

"Yeah," Nick said and sat down. His father took his seat back at his desk. "I know everyone thinks I'm going crazy, but I actually feel better than ever."

His father smiled at him. "You were always such a free-spirited child, but I always held out hope that you would grow up, eventually. Does Lily have anything to do with this?" He arched an eyebrow.

"Everything."

"Good. Your mother and I really like her. Your mother says she is good for you, but these changes have to be what you want too, Nick."

"I know, and they are. I should have made them earlier, but for some reason I didn't. I'm ready now, though."

"Well, I'm glad to hear it. What does Lily make of all this?"

"She doesn't know yet. Dad, she broke up with me when she told me she was pregnant. I was taken aback to say the least, but the biggest mistake I have ever made was letting her and our baby go. I'm going to get everything in place and then tell her. What do you think?"

"I think it's great, and if she is the woman for you, Son, don't let her go. Are you ready to be a father? It's a big responsibility."

"I know," Nick said and was touched by his father's concern. "But I learned from the best, and I'm prepared. Let's get started on the paperwork."

Robert nodded and smiled at Nick. This was good. Another piece of his plan was falling into place. They moved ahead with putting everything in writing.

After his meeting with his father, the next thing Nick had to do was go see his brother Colin. He had an idea what transpired between him and Lily at his parent's place, but he wanted to clear up any misunderstanding. He walked unannounced into his office.

"Hey, brother," Colin said. He smiled and got up from his desk to shake hands. "What are you doing here? I thought you were still out on the Moonlight Queen."

"No," he said. "I came back to meet with Dad and sort some things out. But I stopped by here to talk about Lily."

"Lily who?"

"Lily. The girl I brought to meet the family last month. Do you remember, or were you too drunk?"

"Oh her, yeah. She was hot, but not your usual type. I was drinking, but I do remember giving her some valuable advice on the Becket men."

"What advice?" Nick asked.

"You know, about how we don't settle down. I told her to take it easy and enjoy being, what did I call her? Oh yeah, the flavor of the month."

"You said what?" His anger was rising to the breaking point. No wonder Lily had been so upset.

"What's the big deal?" Colin said, not picking up

on Nick's rage.

"This," Nick said as he lost control and punched Colin square in the face. "Is the big deal. And if you ever talk to my girl like that again, I won't stop with one hit." And then he turned to leave. Colin was gaping at him and holding his jaw as he stormed out of the office without further comment. Nick had a lot to do, and he didn't want to waste a minute.

****

The next two weeks sped by in a blur, and now it was time for Nick to put the finishing touches on his plan. This would be the hardest part, but it just had to work. He had everything riding on this.

He showed up at Victoria's workplace late one afternoon. He had gotten all the information on her whereabouts from the private investigator he had hired.

Walking into the quaint shop that sold candles, lotions, and gift items, the bell above the door rang.

"Be right with you," called a voice from the back of the store.

Nick paced around near the front counter, his nerves frayed to the breaking point. Just then, a petite woman with long black hair in a ponytail was making her way to the front of the store. She was dressed casually in jeans and a red sweater. She had a smile on her face, but as she got closer, the smile faded and turned into a look of pure anger. She had clearly recognized him from the photos Lily had taken when they were together.

"Nick," Victoria said. "What the hell are you doing here?"

"Victoria, please, give me five minutes of your time, and I will tell you everything."

She viewed him with a look of disdain and mistrust. Nick couldn't blame her, after what he had done to her best friend. He was anxious and worried that she wouldn't give him a chance to explain himself, but then she looked him straight in the eye. It was almost as if she was looking right through him, into his soul.

"Okay," she said and looked at her watch. "This better be good. Go."

Chapter Ten

His visit with Victoria had been half an hour ago. Now he was standing just inside the café, looking at Lily curled up by the fireplace, reading a paperback novel. She was gorgeous. His memory of her didn't do her justice. She was dressed in tights and a blue tunic. Her hair was loose and flowing down her back. How could he have let her get away? Well, everything was all about to change, right now.

He went up to the counter and ordered a coffee. He didn't want to look like he was just loitering about, which he was. Thanking the older gentleman behind the counter, he prepared to make his way over to her. Nick took a deep breath, paused, and walked over to where she was sitting.

"Excuse me," he said. "Is this seat taken?" He gestured to the place beside her.

"Oh, I'm sorry…" Then she looked up at him. Her huge green eyes got wider than he had ever seen them. "Nick," she said as she let out a long exhale. "What are you doing here?"

"Hi, Lily," he said. "Can I sit down?"

"I don't know if that's a good idea." A frown and a look of confusion clouded her beautiful face.

"Lily," he said as panic rose in him. "I need to explain some things to you. And if you never want to see me again after this, I will honor your wishes and walk away. But please…" He sounded like he was begging, but he couldn't help himself. "Just give me one more chance."

She stared at him for so long he was sure he'd aged a few years before she answered. She owed him nothing, but maybe if she still had feelings for him deep down, she would listen.

"Well, I don't have a lot of time. I'm meeting Victoria soon…"

Okay, it was time to be honest with her, starting with that.

"Victoria's not coming, Lily. I went to see her at the store earlier today. She told me where I could find you, and I rushed right over here to see you. I hope I'm not too late."

"What?"

"Look," he said. "Don't get mad at Victoria. Will you please come for a drive with me and listen to what I have to say?" He wanted to show her something, and the idea of speaking to her in public did not appeal to him. If he had to, though, he would tell her everything right in the middle of the café.

Nick watched Lily look around. The place was somewhat crowded at this time of day, and he hoped she agreed that they should speak in private.

"All right," she said, after a long few moments. She stood up and gathered her things. It was then Nick noticed the slight swell of her belly. The baby, their baby, was growing inside her. This plan had to work, not just for his sake anymore.

****

Lily followed Nick out to his car. He headed over to a large SUV parked in the lot. It was the same sapphire blue as his sports car, but the similarities ended there. "What's this?"

"Oh. I traded my other car in. It doesn't suit me anymore." He opened the passenger side door for her. "Here," he said as he held out his hand for her. "I think you'll find this much more comfortable."

"Nick," she said. Her voice was full of suspicion. "What is going on?"

"I promise I'll explain everything when we get there."

"Get where?"

"Just trust me. I know it's a lot to ask. But Victoria approves, if that helps."

"Okay," she said without further comment. She got into the vehicle herself, ignoring his hand. Her head was full of questions. She hadn't expected to see him again. He was still the same handsome captain she had met a few short months ago, but something in him had changed. She couldn't quite figure out what. His hair was freshly cut in that short crewcut she liked, and his blue eyes shone.

Would the baby look like him? *Stop it. It didn't matter.* He was probably just here to try and buy her off or something. If that were the case, he could have sent his lawyer, couldn't he? Maybe the lawyer needed to see them both in person or something like that. Oh well, she would know soon enough, and she made a mental note to have a stern talk with Victoria.

The car was comfortable, but she didn't feel like talking to Nick while they were driving. It was not worth the risk of them getting into an accident if they started to argue and he got distracted. She'd been waiting a month to talk to him again, she could wait a bit longer.

He put on some soft classical music, not his usual radio station, but he wasn't acting anything like himself. She looked out the window for a while and noticed they were getting on the highway.

Then she closed her eyes. She shouldn't do that, but she was so tired and Nick was making no effort at conversation. The pregnancy although it was going well, left her tired all the time, and she had been so busy trying to put her life back together, she wasn't sleeping as much as she should.

She awoke with a start and looked at her watch. An hour had passed, and the car had stopped. What time was it? Where were they? She looked up and recognized Nick's condo at once.

"What are we doing at your place, Nick?"

"Lily, just come inside with me." He got out of the vehicle and rushed over to open her door for her. She didn't get out of the car.

"What are you, so rich that your lawyer makes house calls?" She couldn't help but blurt the question out.

"What? What lawyer?" he asked. "Never mind. Come inside, it's getting cold out here." He offered his hand again to help her out of the vehicle, but she didn't take it. She wasn't going to start relying on him now.

Nick looked puzzled by her behavior, but he didn't comment. He just led the way through the opulent lobby decorated in rich burgundy and black furniture. It had gorgeous silver mirrors and other accents.

The concierges at the front desk hopped up and rushed over to greet them.

"Welcome back, Captain Becket. Can I help you

with anything today?"

"No, thank you, Joshua. Actually yes, can you please make sure no one disturbs me until further notice?"

"Of course, sir," the young man said. Nick slipped him a fifty-dollar bill, and Lily almost gasped out loud. Does he buy everyone off? Well, she'd already told him she couldn't be bought. She was just going to have to repeat herself when they got upstairs.

Nick walked over to the open elevator door and inserted the key for the penthouse. It was the longest ride of Lily's life. She should have just told Nick to have his lawyer call her lawyer. Except she didn't have one and couldn't afford the expense right now. Finally, the elevator reached the top floor.

Lily stepped off and was flooded with memories of the last time she and Nick were here together. They had been so happy, and she had spent most of the week in his strong and comforting embrace. *Stop it. You've made so much progress getting over him, don't slide backward now.*

She looked around the foyer, and it looked the same, but as she entered the living room, the glass tables and expensive leather sofas were gone. They had been replaced with sturdy looking wood tables and overstuffed comfortable sofas and chairs in muted pastels. This was weird. Nick was looking at her, waiting for a response. Okay, so he had redecorated, big deal. Did he actually want her opinion? It still looked elegant of course, but somehow more like a home than a bachelor pad.

"The place looks great, Nick," she said, not sure why it mattered whether she liked it or not. "Where's your lawyer?"

"Come and sit down," he said and gestured to the sofa. "And why do you keep mentioning my lawyer?"

She took a seat. It was as comfortable as it looked. What was that in the corner of the room, near the terrace doors? Was it a rocking chair? She ignored it for now. "Your lawyer, Nick, the one who is going to sweep this whole mess under the carpet for you. But I've already told you, I don't want your money."

"Did you think I brought you here to meet with my lawyer? No, Lily, that couldn't be further from the truth."

"Well, what is the truth, Nick? I think I've waited long enough. If you haven't noticed, I'm pregnant, and I tire very easily. You've now driven me halfway across the state, not to see your lawyer apparently, so why?"

If he didn't start talking, she was going to run screaming from the room. He took a seat and looked deep into her eyes.

"Lily, until I met you, I was just a player. I'm sure that was obvious to you. I treated women well, but they never really meant anything to me. I wasn't serious about my life and spent most of my time partying. When we started dating, it was a whole new world for me. And it was great, but it was a big adjustment for me. I was on the right path with you and hoped way down the road we would get married and have kids, but I didn't expect a baby so soon."

"Nick," Lily interrupted him.

"No, Lily, please, let me finish."

She nodded, and he went on.

"I was in a state of shock and panic when you told me you were pregnant. I said and did everything wrong, and I will regret that for the rest of my life. But after you left, there was a hole in my heart without you. It's a big void that can't be filled by anything or anyone else. I think I had to lose you to see this fact, and I did. Ever since then, I have been working to make amends for the pain I have caused you."

He got up and pulled a small box from his pocket. Kneeling down beside her, he looked up at her with his brilliant blue eyes and then he said it.

"I love you, Lily Kingston, with all my heart and soul. Will you marry me?"

He opened the box to reveal a sparkling two-carat diamond ring. It was a round shape set in white gold. Lily gasped when she saw the elegant, beautiful piece of jewelry.

"Oh, Nick," she said and tears filled her eyes. She had waited months for this moment, but she just couldn't see how it would work.

"I love you too. I always will, but it's just not going to work, what with you on the ship most of the time and me in Orchard Park."

"I resigned from the ship, Lily," he said.

"You did what?"

"I quit. I promoted Daniel to captain, and I'm going to help my dad run the business. He needs my help. I was planning to make the move, eventually, but now I know the timing is right. We can be together. I fixed up this place to make it more like somewhere you would want to live. Or we can buy a house in Orchard Park if you don't like it here."

"Nick, this is crazy. You can't give up your job as captain and redecorate just for me. This isn't what you want for your life. You need to be free. I'm sure of that."

"No, Lily, this is exactly what I want. I've never been so sure of anything in my entire life. My job, this condo…they mean nothing to me if I don't have you by my side. You have made some great sacrifices yourself by quitting the job you loved on the ship, all to come back to where you started and raise our baby. I can't, I won't and don't want you to do that alone. I want to be with you. You and our baby, always.

"And I want to show you one more thing before you answer my question." He put the ring back in his pocket. "Come with me."

Lily's head was spinning. Quit his job? Fixed up his beloved condo for her? He said he loved her, and so far, his actions were proving it. She took his hand as he led her down the hallway. This was almost too much for her.

"Nick," she said as he stopped at the door to his spare room. She remembered this was his office; she didn't need to see it again.

"No, don't say anything until you see it," he whispered in her ear as he eased open the door. Sunlight was streaming through the mint green curtains. Wait a minute, there were masculine wooden blinds on the window last time she was in here. The walls were now a matching green with a beautiful mural of a forest on one wall. There was a crib in one corner and changing table and dresser in the other. They were all made from solid oak. The room was fully furnished; all that was missing was a baby.

"I did the room in green, the color of your eyes. And the color also works for a boy or a girl since I don't know what we're having." Nick stopped talking.

He was studying Lily, waiting for her response. He had said everything she had wanted to hear. This was truly the happiest moment of her life. She looked up into his radiant blue eyes, the eyes that had mesmerized her from the first day she met him.

She threw herself into his arms, clung to him, and cried. She saw tears in Nick's eyes as well, and she was overcome with emotion.

"I love you, Nicholas Becket, and I would be honored to become your wife."

He sighed a sound of pure relief, took her in his arms, and leaned down to kiss her. "I love you too, Mrs. Lily Becket." Her kiss was passion filled with all the longing she had stored up for him in the past few weeks. Their lips parted, but he still held her tight. "Here, put this on and let's make it official." He took the ring out of the box and slipped it on her finger. It was a perfect fit. They were both smiling and crying now, but this time it was tears of joy.

"Oh and, Nick," she said and patted her stomach. "It's a boy."

He looked surprised at first, then smiled and bent down to put an ear to her middle. "Hello, baby boy," he said to the slight bulge in her belly. "You are going to have the best mom and dad in the world, and we will love you forever."

Lily laughed. "I'm not sure he can hear you."

"Yes he can, and I'm glad he was here to witness the beginning of the rest of our lives."

"Me too."

Then he stood, lifting her off her feet and into his strong embrace.

"What now?" she asked as he cradled her in his

arms.

"Oh, Lily," he said. "I've missed you more than you will ever know, and we have a lot of catching up to do."

He carried her across the hall to the master bedroom. As they crossed the threshold into the room, he whispered to her. "And I can't wait another minute to start our new life in paradise…together."

A word about the author...

After writing more essays than she could count while completing her university studies, Kate Randle decided to swap out the world of academic prose for something more exciting: romance novels.

Her first book, *In Pursuit of Paradise* encompasses all of the things she loves the most: sun, sand, and the ocean. Because these things are often in short supply in her native Canada, she frequently travels south in order to get her vitamin D fix.

Kate lives near Toronto, Ontario, with her incredibly supportive husband and kids. Two adorable rescue felines round out her family to keep things interesting and covered in cat hair.

For more information, please visit Kate at her website:
www.katerandle.com

Thank you for purchasing
this publication of The Wild Rose Press, Inc.

If you enjoyed the story, we would appreciate your
letting others know by leaving a review.

For other wonderful stories,
please visit our on-line bookstore at
www.thewildrosepress.com.

For questions or more information
contact us at
info@thewildrosepress.com.

The Wild Rose Press, Inc.
www.thewildrosepress.com

Stay current with The Wild Rose Press, Inc.

Like us on Facebook

https://www.facebook.com/TheWildRosePress

And Follow us on Twitter
https://twitter.com/WildRosePress